CASSID

Diana Pullein-Thompson gre_____
four children. They all learne____
and, their first mount was Co_____ polo pony,
whom they used to climb on to by stepladder. Diana left school
at fourteen, and, with her two sisters, started the Grove Riding
School, which inspired some of her early books and eventually
grew into a large establishment with forty-two horses and
ponies. She has written over twenty-five books, and her sisters,
Christine and Josephine, are also well-known as popular
children's writers. She is married to art historian, Dennis Farr,
and they live in London with their two children and a dog. They
also have a grey mare called Bianca, a cream pony called
Muffin and Muffin's son, Stowaway.

Other titles by Diana Pullein-Thompson in Armada

CASSIDY
IN DANGER

DIANA PULLEIN-THOMPSON

Armada

Cassidy in Danger was first published in the U.K.
in 1979 by J. M. Dent & Sons Ltd.
This edition was first published in Armada in
1981 by Fontana Paperbacks, 14 St. James's Place,
London SW1A 1PS

© Diana Pullein-Thompson 1979

Printed in Great Britain by
Love & Malcomson Ltd.,
Brighton Road, Redhill, Surrey.

CONTENTS

*With love to Benedict, who also owned
a rat of singular charm and character.*

CHAPTER ONE

LOST ON THE RAILWAY

"Come back," I said, "and don't take risks."

"Oh Katie!" my mother laughed, "you are speaking like a parent, reversing the roles. Of course I'll come back. Don't worry. Enjoy yourself. Have lots of splendid rides. Get off at Birmingham International."

The whistle blew. I kissed her on the cheek. She smelt of almond soap. The train started to glide out of the station.

"Be good Katerina! Help Patsy with the washing-up," my mother began to wave.

There was an ache in the pit of my stomach as her hand grew smaller. She became a small brown figure; brown-haired, brown-eyed, sun-tanned in a brown, flowered skirt and brown top open at the throat. I couldn't see the bracelets on her arms or the yellow amber beads around her neck, but I knew they were there.

"Enjoy Russia," I called, leaning out. "Give my love to him . . ." I couldn't say Dad or Father, the words died on my tongue, because I couldn't believe in a man I had never seen.

I stopped waving as the platform slid from view. I went to a seat, put my case in the rack above and sat down opposite an Asian family. I was going to the Midlands to stay with Patsy Cooper, my Godmother, whom I hadn't seen since I was two, although she had sent me a pound every Christmas. Patsy was an antique dealer, a war widow, who had befriended us years ago, when my homeless, jobless mother had wandered back from Eastern Europe with a baby in her arms.

Patsy had written that there was a riding school near her lodge, where I could probably help with the ponies, bringing them up from the fields, mucking out and perhaps schooling them a bit, as I had gained experience during the last summer holidays on a farm in Cumbria. We had rented a cottage there amongst the hills and my mother had worked in a shop selling pottery to tourists. Our land-lord, a widowed farmer, had been immensely kind, letting me ride his ponies and taking us out in his Land Rover. I had fallen in love with the grey crags, the silent hills, the tumbling streams, and a little bit with the farmer, too, who seemed to know so much about horses and cattle and the folklore of the fells. But now, sitting in the train, I was full of doubts. A riding school would be very different from that lonely farmstead. It would be well regulated and run on rules that had to be obeyed; there would be notices that I might not understand. My flaws would soon be obvious even to the most junior assistant, but my mother had made me sound an expert.

"She really has quite a flair, a natural rider, sits a horse like someone on a Greek frieze. She has a special affinity with animals and, what's more, she's pony mad," she had informed Patsy, sitting on the stairs in the house where we had lived in a bed-sitter, the black telephone's cable stretched to its limit so that she could hold its headpiece to her ear.

It was July now and soon I saw a procession of cars glinting like tin toys on a motorway and lorries and, now and then, a coach with faces at windows, and then we were passing through flat fields dotted here and there with houses or villages. It looked hot outside but the train was air-conditioned so that I couldn't be sure. The Asian man disappeared for a few moments and came back with Pepsi Cola for his family. My mother had given me a five-pound note, but I didn't want to fritter that away on drinks and sweets. Besides I reckoned I might wish to buy Patsy a present since she was being kind enough to house and feed me for six weeks. "Small, dark, bespectacled and tough as old boots. Speaks her mind and calls a spade a spade," had been my mother's description of my Godmother. "And she doesn't approve of me. She thinks I've messed up my life through lack of planning and attention. She says I drift from one disaster to another while my talents shrivel from want of use," my mother had laughed, because she doesn't care about what other people think of her. But I had taken note and wondered whether Patsy would judge me equally severely.

8

Now, to stop myself worrying, I turned my mind to the riding school allowing my imagination to take over. I saw a well ordered yard, white boxes with green doors, noble heads looking out with pricked ears and shining eyes, a dog lying in the sun warming her stomach, and a tall blonde girl welcoming me.

"We've heard all about you. Welcome, Katie. Let me introduce you to the horses first. Now this is the pony we have allotted to you—Silver."

A dapple grey leaned forward to sniff my coat.

"He needs experience," the girl went on, "so he's yours for the summer holidays."

"Do you think I'm good enough?"

"Katie, if you can ride fell ponies you can ride anything," the blonde in my day-dream smiled as she patted my shoulder re-assuringly.

As the train raced on into leafy Warwickshire my fantasy grew, spreading out its tentacles like convolvulus, hanging on every shred of hope that I had allowed myself when looking into my future.

I was at a show receiving a red rosette from a charming woman in a trouser suit when the train stopped, and slamming doors jerked me back into reality.

"Coventry, this is Coventry," a voice boomed.

"Not you?" asked the Asian looking at me with his peat-dark eyes.

"No, Birmingham," I said, smiling as I pushed back my fantasy which had become so much more real than reality.

"Ah, Birmingham, another half hour. We go to Wolverhampton." My mother always talks to people in trains, but had warned me against speaking to strangers, so I went back to my show ring, where cameras clicked as I cantered my lovely grey round for all the onlookers to see, the red rosette grasped between my teeth.

Outside the real skies paled to tapioca grey; the fields were flat again, parted mostly by barbed wire, spoiled by ugly houses and unkempt sheds. It wasn't real country, much indeed was wasteland. Presently we came to more buildings, flat-roofed like cardboard boxes; a treeless car park shone hot and black in the afternoon sun. The train slowed down, a concrete road curled away, between huge light standards, along which an empty blue and cream bus sped like something in a film; another car park could now be glimpsed, with rows of cars of all colours. People passed through our carriage. Doors slammed shut again. With difficulty I pushed the grey pony into the back of my mind.

"Birmingham International. No?" enquired the Asian. "Birmingham!"

I stared wildly out of the window. "Are you sure?" I had imagined a town with tall grey buildings and people pushing and thrusting. I found my suitcase. The Asian sprang to his feet.

"Too late, I think," he said. "Do not try to jump."

The train began to slide forward as I rushed to the nearest door and looked for a handle; then I saw that I must open the window and put out my hand to grasp it from outside.

"Too late, much too late," said the Asian at my elbow, smelling of spice and strange herbs.

I began to sweat as the train slid away past the platform, where a bespectacled woman waved at me frantically, like a distracted owl.

The Asian said: "Sit down. Come back. There is no more to be done now. You will go to New Street Station, Birmingham and catch a train back."

"But that didn't look like Birmingham," I wailed. "It wasn't a town. It was a sort of factory."

"O.K., O.K., don't worry. It was an Exhibition Centre," replied the Asian soothingly. "Maybe, you do want Birmingham itself. Let me see your ticket, please."

I stopped biting my nails to dig into my pocket and produce it for him. I felt dreadful.

The Asian put on a pair of spectacles.

"No, no," he said sadly. "You are right. It is clearly printed here, Birmingham International."

He turned to speak to his wife in their own language, then, looking at me again, he explained that we had just left the first new station to be built in Britain for fifty years.

"It is no factory. It is to serve the National Exhibition Centre. I do not think you were attending. I do not think young women like yourself should travel alone. In my country things are different. But then many of the women

10

cannot read. But for you this time it is only half an hour lost and what is half an hour out of a lifetime?"

"Yes, that's right," I said, cheered a little, putting my hands in my lap. "I mustn't make a mountain out of a molehill." His philosophy was, I thought, similar to my mother's: don't worry over small things, a train missed is a nuisance not a calamity, a lost glove or pound an inconvenience rather than a disaster. "We must keep our sense of proportion," had been her constant cry as we had moved from one uncomfortable lodging to another. "We are lucky to have beds to sleep in and a plate of food to eat. Think of the starving in India, the tortured in Cambodia and the Dissidents in the Soviet Union. How they suffer compared with us!"

Now the train raced through suburbs, to the town where tower blocks rose up like sugar cubes to meet the summer sky, shabby factories stood next to scrap yards, with broken cars lying in twisted heaps, waiting for some machine to crush them into small usable pieces. To the left were partly gutted houses standing in rows like toothless people waiting for death and, next to them, new, bright, boxy terraced cottages with little windows like Chinese eyes, and walled backyards. It was all very different from the scenes which had grown in my imagination.

"Now this is Birmingham itself," said the Asian getting up as the train slowed down and stopped. "I will open the door for you. Tell the ticket collector what has happened. It will not be a new experience for him. Others have made the same mistake."

"The trouble is that I make more mistakes than most people," I said. "Thank you very much. I hope you have a good journey to Wolverhampton."

"Just one stop, only minutes," replied the Asian handing me down my suitcase. "You will be all right."

"Four-ten, platform number seven," said the ticket collector when I had explained my predicament.

Coming out on the concourse I saw a clock that told me it was a quarter to four. I felt my five-pound note again. Should I break into it and stand myself a bar of chocolate? No, I decided, then I should be cluttered up with ten-penny pieces and crumpled pound notes, which would not in any way compensate me for cashing the first fiver I had been given in my life. I sat down on a seat, watched the people going to and fro, and the digital clock moving, and I tried to remember which television programmes would be on that evening. A nasal voice started to speak over a loudspeaker, breaking into my thoughts.

"Katerina Turgenieff, will Katerina Turgenieff please go to the Station Manager's office?"

"Me?" For a moment my heart hammered, then I felt relief. Well then, I decided, I had better not catch the train back, for obviously the efficient Patsy Cooper had acted. I jumped to my feet, stopped a homely looking woman, who was hurrying by dragging a reluctant toddler.

"Where is it, please?"

"What, dear?"

"The Station Manager's office. I am Katerina Turgenieff and they are calling me over the loudspeaker."

For a moment I felt important, but the woman cut me down to size saying:

"Well, it's over there, isn't it? Can't you see the notice, large as life?" She pointed to a brown door with writing on it. "That's the Station Manager's office, that is. Now I'm in a hurry, love, if you don't mind."

I went through the brown door and then a glass door, where a pale man in rimless glasses asked if he could help me.

"I'm Katerina Turgenieff," I said, more sheepishly this time.

"Good, that's great. You've turned up. Sit down, please." He pointed to a chair. "Your Godmother is doing her nut over you. I've been instructed to ring her back, so hang on. She'll be over to fetch you, takes half an hour, nothing to worry about."

"I'm sorry to have been such a nuisance. The other station didn't look international."

"It's easily done. You'd got your nose in a book I expect, Georgette Heyer or Agatha Christie, or dreaming about some pop star. Trains don't stop long at stations these days. I've got a teenage daughter myself, so I know what you youngsters are like."

He went away into a back room to telephone, while I

started to bite my nails again. Would Patsy be angry? Would she shout at me in front of other people? My mother had described her as downright, a woman who spoke her mind. That could mean a row. I started to sweat again. The man came back, and saying: "Catch," tossed me a packet of Polos.

"To aid the digestion," he added, laughing. "Want a cup of tea?"

Half an hour later Patsy Cooper stood in the doorway, wearing jeans and a brown sweater, a slim figure with a smile that showed slightly crooked teeth.

"Oh Katie! I'm sorry. Bad luck! I should have warned you especially that there were two Birmingham stations," she cried, then relaxing into her normal matter-of-fact voice, she continued: "Were you very worried? I thought I caught a glimpse of you at a door as the train hurried on its journey." Her concerned brown eyes searched my face from behind large glasses; her forehead furrowed. I noticed that she had a small mole on her left cheek and that her hands were freckled like a pheasant's egg.

"No," I said. "No, I'm all right, thank you. I should have realized. Thank you for coming, thank you very much. I'm sorry I made the mistake."

"Not to worry. Where's your knapsack? Let's go!"

Now she became not only matter of fact, but brisk—the real Patsy I was to know so well as the weeks passed.

"I've got a suitcase, I'm afraid. It's very light."

"A suitcase. Good heavens, it's the first time I've known your mother to own such a thing!" said Patsy. "Now have you thanked this nice man for looking after you?"

"Thank you so much," I said, looking straight at the pale eyes behind the rimless glasses.

"You're welcome. But I wouldn't do it again if I were you. Once is enough. Look at the names of the stations next time."

Within minutes we were racing out of Birmingham in Patsy's small orange car. "I'm dreadfully sorry," I said.

"I hear you like horses," she said.

"Yes, I want to work with them when I'm grown up."

"Splendid, nice to meet someone who knows her mind.

13

Such a change! Well, there's a riding school in the village and I expect they could do with a bit of help. Actually, I hope they'll adopt you, because I'm out all day, chasing after tables and chairs, stained glass, old street lights and what-nots. You'll be on your own quite a lot, but your mother says you're pretty self-reliant. She says you knew how to toast a crumpet by the time you were six and to scramble an egg a year later."

I thought of the bottoms of three saucepans I had burned and of the large green dinner plate I had broken last week and said nothing.

"You'll have to fend for yourself a bit," Patsy went on, "but at thirteen you should manage pretty well. I mean you're a teenager, aren't you? Teenagers these days are grown up, responsible, almost adult."

"Yes, I can cope. I won't be a nuisance," I said.

"I didn't mean that, I was worrying about you not me," said Patsy, as we shot past Birmingham Airport.

CHAPTER TWO

FENDING FOR MYSELF

The riding school was half a mile from the lodge house where Patsy lived, right in the centre of the village, near the church and the little river which gurgled under a red brick bridge.

As I drew near my steps slowed down. I was frightened, because I was going to ask a favour, a chance to help, and no one likes asking favours of those they do not know. And if the owners of the school didn't want my help, Patsy would be in a dilemma, because she had settled in her own mind that I should spend the best part of the summer holidays there. I felt horribly embarrassed. Then I remembered my five-pound note and decided, with relief, that I could book a riding lesson first and then feel my way before asking to help.

I turned up the driveway in better heart. To my left three ponies grazed diligently in a paddock; ahead of me an outside school led my eye on to a row of looseboxes with rather ugly asbestos roofs, and then a garden fronting a red brick bungalow.

A crossbred collie came barking down the driveway, then greeted me with wagging tail and lowered body. A girl wheeling a barrow of manure stopped.

"Can I help?"

"I'm Katie Turgenieff, I'm staying with Patsy Cooper at the lodge, and I wonder whether I can book a ride?"

The girl had short, dark hair cut into a fringe and a beaky nose. She wore jeans and wellington boots and a denim shirt.

"Come along, I'll look in the book. Miss Kirk is out just now. Can you ride?"

"A bit," I said.

"Walk, trot, canter, gallop?"

"Yes, I can jump a bit too, up to three feet, but I'm not very experienced."

"It's two pounds fifty a lesson," she said opening the book.

"Oh," I answered, feeling my fiver. "Is it possible to work here in exchange for riding lessons?"

"Not really. It depends on Miss Kirk of course. It's her decision not mine."

"I've ridden in the fell country, you know—Cumbria, on a lovely black fell pony called Captain, and a mare called Destiny. I've ridden all day and jumped streams, and obstacles I've put up in the fields, but I haven't actually been taught."

"You are bound to have lots of faults then," said the girl discouragingly. "Of course the schools haven't broken up yet round here, so we've no proper classes until the weekend. Would you like individual tuition? You may need it if you've taught yourself. That's three pounds an hour."

"Couldn't you just give me a lesson now, just half an hour, or couldn't we go for a ride or something? I can't afford more than two pounds. I mean I have five, but that's got to last me till halfway through September when my mother comes back from Russia. It's all a bit complicated—she's gone there to see my father . . ." Suddenly

15

I wanted to pour out all my anxieties, but the girl put down the book and looked at me curiously.

"Come down to earth," she said. "Why not get Mrs. Cooper to ring up and book the ride?"

"No, no, she sent me to do it," I said quickly, feeling I had let my tongue run away. "What about tomorrow?"

"There's no class till Friday evening. Don't you have to go to school? I mean you are not sixteen, are you? You don't look it."

"No, I've been allowed a fortnight off, because of Russia you see."

"Well, Friday evening at five-thirty then," said the girl writing in the book, "and people who don't cancel twelve hours in advance are charged the full two pounds fifty."

"Which pony will I be riding?" I asked, looking longingly at a grey with dark eyes and pink muzzle.

"Miss Kirk decides that. She rules this place with a rod of iron, actually, so don't tell her any funny stories about Russia. She might go up the spout. She's old-fashioned. And, by the way, I advise you to buy a hairnet for your hair. She likes people properly dressed."

"All right, Friday at five-thirty," I said, patting the dog who was licking my hand. "Thank you very much."

I walked even more slowly back to Patsy's house which stands by a gate at the entrance to a park, and sat a long time in the garden stroking her fat tabby cat, which is called Felix. She hadn't warned me about Miss Kirk and the hairnet and, for a while, I felt very let-down, and I wanted my mother, because she would have turned my talk with the girl into a joke. As it was, I sank into what my mother calls one of my "Russian depressions," and saw six weeks of boredom and loneliness, lying ahead of me like a long wet march to a lost battle.

The cat purred and gazed into my face with large, sleepy, green eyes. I wondered whether my mother was now in Moscow talking to my father who was, according to his photograph, a bear of a man, tall, burly and bearded with a wide, pleasant face and blue, far-seeing eyes. My mother had said they would meet in a park and sit and talk under the trees, and exchange gifts. She had made it all sound very romantic, but then she made everything sound exciting. She was an optimist and probably pictured me now singing as I groomed a pony at the school, or chatting merrily to Patsy as we sat in deck chairs under a magnolia tree. My mother, I decided, was impractical and that was why she got into so many difficulties.

"Damn it," I said to Felix. "I feel like crying."

I looked across the garden as I spoke, to the iron palings that parted it from a field adjoining the park, and then I noticed for the first time a bay pony watching me from under a forelock of black hair. "Who are you?" I said. And he raised his head another inch and whinnied softly. After gently putting the cat down on the lawn, I went across to the fence and held out a hand. The pony came across with a long, easy stride, his little pointed ears pricked and his eyes shining with expectation.

"I haven't anything to give you."

He nuzzled the pockets of my jeans.

"You're lonely like me. Are you a failure, too? You don't look that way." I patted his sleek neck, ran my fingers through his dark mane and he rubbed his head against my shoulder. And I felt suddenly at home, as I always do with ponies.

"It's a question of reincarnation," my mother had once said, when I had explained this feeling to her. "You were probably a pony last time, or maybe a cat or dog who lived with ponies. That's why you don't yet feel at home with humans. You're a new soul in human form."

Presently I went into Patsy's kitchen and took a carrot from the vegetable rack, cut it into long slices, and fed it to the pony, who ate it neatly without snatching.

Patsy came back at lunch time, because, she said, it was my first day and I needed to settle in before I was left alone. We scrambled eggs and ate them, with a handful of cress and part of a sliced green pepper, in the garden.

"Who does the pony belong to?" I asked, pointing.

"Oh, that's Cassidy. It's a sad story and he hasn't long for this world."

"What do you mean? He's not going to be destroyed?"

"I am afraid so," said Patsy, calmly munching cress.

"But it's not possible. He's young and beautiful and sweet. Is he ill or lame or what?" I sounded aggressive and

17

was surprised how fiercely protective I felt. My eyes probably blazed.

"Now keep calm, don't over-react," said Patsy, her little
crooked teeth working away. "He throws everyone, disas-
trously and deliberately. He was bought for the lovely
Arabella, who lives in the big house. She wins all the cups
round here at the local shows, and she wanted to break
and school a pony as a sort of new experience. But in a
trice he had broken her arm so badly that it had to be
pinned. Then the expert, George Pratt, who has schooled
more youngsters than he cares to remember, took over,
only to land in the grass with a dislocated hip. Then Miss
Kirk, bless her, came to the rescue, offering the services of
her new instructress who had just taken those advanced
British Horse Society tests, or whatever it is, and the little
devil concussed her for a week. Then Sir Stanley Petworth
said enough was enough, and the pony must be shot
before he damaged anyone else. But Arabella pleaded that
he might have a last summer, so he's here till the autumn
and then he'll go to the hunt kennels to feed hounds."

"And who is the lovely Arabella?" I asked in my
mother's voice.

"Sir Stanley's daughter, an only child. She rides in all
the shows round here. When she took it in her head to
break and school a pony, they bought Cassidy unbroken
at a sale; paid one hundred pounds for him, I'm told."

I looked at the pony and thought of hounds tearing his
flesh and said nothing.

"Did you go to the riding school?" asked Patsy, blinking
at me through her black-framed spectacles.

I gave her an edited version of my visit.

"Miss Kirk does look rather formidable," she said, "but
I gather she has a heart of gold underneath the rugged
exterior. Look, let me pay for the lesson."

"No," I insisted. "Mummy gave me a fiver." I took the
note out of my pocket and waved it in front of Patsy's face.
"See, I'm rich."

"It won't last long," she said.

"Why do you think he chucks people off?"

"Who?"

"Cassidy."

18

"Search me," said Patsy.

"I mean, I watched the farmer we stayed with in the fells when he was breaking a pony, and there was no bucking. He said if a pony bucked it meant you were mishandling things. He said ponies didn't want to chuck off their friends. They only bucked through high spirits or fear. Did Arabella hurry him too much?"

"No, she was out there day after day sending him round in circles on a leash or whatever you call it. At least three weeks passed before she mounted him, and then he was like something out of a Wild West film. No one had seen anything quite like it before. Be an angel, pop in and bring out the bowl of fruit and switch the coffee on, will you."

Eating bananas, we fell silent; the cat purring on Patsy's knee and the bees busy nearby amongst the honeysuckle, which clambered up the lodge in wild abundance. A plane droned overhead and Cassidy left the fence and wandered away unaware, I felt sure, that a death warrant hung over his neat, well-formed head.

"I shall have to leave you now until seven this evening, I'm afraid," Patsy said. "I'm sorry, old thing, but if you need help, there's that cottage just across the garden, see the brick and flint one?" she pointed. "Some theatrical people live there, well, she's a telly personality, I think and he's an actor and they have a son called Matthew. They're rather Bohemian, a bit arty, if you know what I mean, but they'll always help out in an emergency. They're really my nearest neighbours. I used to baby-sit occasionally when they couldn't get anyone else and the boy was smaller. They have a chow, but you needn't be afraid of her, she's gentle as a lamb."

"It's all right, I like dogs," I said.

"And the number of the shop is up above the telephone in my sitting-room, so phone me there if you have any queries. All right?"

"Absolutely," I said.

"And I'm sorry I haven't a telly, but use the radio whenever you like, treat it as your own, and the books too, make yourself at home. Now I must make tracks. Be an angel and wash up, will you?"

"Of course," I said, "and thank you for everything."

"Bye now."

A moment later the orange mini-estate car shot off down the road, and Felix climbed on my knee and started pummelling me with his paws.

After washing up, I spent all the afternoon in the field with Cassidy. I made a rough halter out of a piece of rope I found in Patsy's garage and, after tying him to the fence, groomed him with the toughest of her two clothes brushes. I cleaned out his hoofs as best I could with a bottle opener and talked to him as though he was my best friend. Then I fetched Patsy's radio and tuned into Radio One and watched him while he listened with me to Abba and the Rolling Stones and Queen and other pop groups. He had a shapely white star in the middle of his forehead and one neat white sock on the near hind, otherwise he was bay with black points and as shiny as a polished conker, with a glow of health in his eyes and a perky expression which won my heart.

"They're not going to feed you to hounds. I shall stop them. I don't know how, but I will. There must be an answer. If only you could speak!"

The pony looked at me then with such wide-eyed innocence that I could not believe that there was any viciousness in his nature; then he gently pawed the ground. "Oh, your hoofs," I said. "I forgot to polish them."

I went back to Patsy's neat kitchen and found a bottle of sunflower oil and a cloth and oiled his hoofs. "Perhaps if you are cherished, you'll change," I said, a plan forming in my mind. The widowed farmer had said, "Why should an unbroken pony mind a friend climbing on his back? No reason. No reason at all. If you make friends with the youngsters first you don't run into trouble. Trust and respect are essential. If all trainers understood that there'd be no vicious and spoiled animals." This farmer, whose name was Justin Appleby, had handled his animals with loving care, firmly yet gently, and his voice had been soft when he spoke to them in an accent that belonged to the fells. I wished that he was here now standing beside me with my mother, and giving me his advice with all the confidence gained from wide experience. He was, I thought, a man who always seemed to know what to do.

He had even made my mother practical during the six weeks we had rented his cottage. And he had been immeasurably kind to us, driving us around in his Land Rover showing us local beauty spots and other wilder places unknown to visitors. On the last evening he had taken us out to dinner at a pub which served garlic bread with beetroot soup and steak in a wine and mushroom sauce, and a wonderful pudding made of cream, sponge fingers and rum.

"Mr. Appleby would not have allowed you to get into this predicament," I told Cassidy, as he looked across the garden at Felix who was climbing a mulberry tree. "It's somebody's silly fault, not yours." I ran my hands down his legs and rubbed him behind his ears.

Later that evening, when Patsy was back, I helped get supper.

"We're having ham and salad, yoghurt and biscuits and cheese. I'm a bit of a health crank about food," she said. "Fetch the oil and vinegar and I'll show you how to make a delicious dressing, and a bit of garlic too, it's on top of the fridge."

"Goodness," she said on my return. "I hadn't realized I was so near the bottom of the sunflower bottle. Put sunflower oil on that shopping list on the dresser, would you? And get the paprika—it's in the herbs-and-spices rack."

She started to pour oil into a bowl and then stopped. "There's grit in it. Heavens, that's not very hygienic. We'd better throw that away."

Watching her face, I blushed. Then she looked at me.

"You haven't been drinking the oil or something have you, or did you use it as sun tan mixture? Come on, own up, Katie. I won't bite your head right off this time." She looked like an angry owl now, deprived of his dinner.

"Hoofs," I said quietly. "Cassidy's hoofs."

Patsy's eyebrows went up. "You mean you've used this, my best sunflower oil from the health store at sixty-nine pence a bottle to polish that pony's feet, Katie?"

"I'm sorry," I muttered remorsefully. "I was over-enthusiastic. I've got five pounds, I'll buy another bottle, tomorrow."

"But you can't get it here. I buy it from the health store in Solihull. Oh really, Katie, it's a bit much isn't it?"

I thought of the hairs on her best clothes brush and nodded.

"I'll give you the sixty pence. I can afford it."

"No, no I won't allow that. After all it's only half a bottle wasted. Here, you had better have the rest for that wretched pony, since it's no longer fit for human consumption," she tossed the plastic bottle to me. "But please don't take anything else without asking first."

"No, I promise," I said.

"I know you've had rather an odd upbringing, but there are simple normal rules of behaviour which we must all abide by if we are not to go back to a jungle state."

"Yes, I know, I'm sorry," I said. "I won't help myself to anything else."

"And the radio, where's that? I like to listen to the eight o'clock news summary, while I have supper."

"Oh, it's in the garden," I confessed miserably. "I'm sorry, I was playing it to Cassidy. I thought it might make him relax and instil confidence."

"You're a very strange child," said Patsy, cutting up a lettuce with scissors. "I think we shall have to abandon the dressing. Never mind, there's a bit of mayonnaise, that'll have to do. Now take the ham through into the dining-room. And please remember that all the furniture in this house is valuable, every chair, table, bench or knick-knack. Don't put hot things down without a mat underneath. Then fetch the radio."

"I'll always eat my lunch in the garden," I said.

"Well, I'm hoping you'll be able to take sandwiches to the riding school, soon," said Patsy Cooper. "Come on, cheer up, old thing, we'll soon make you civilized."

"I'll just go and get the radio," I said. "And see what Cassidy is doing. He's a very sweet pony."

CHAPTER THREE

A RIDING LESSON

The next day I taught Cassidy to shake hands and I leaned across his back, putting a little weight on his spine. His ears went back, but he didn't move, so I gave him a slice of carrot. I groomed him again and led him round the field making him stop to a light pressure on the rope and move on at my command. I thought if I taught him absolute obedience he might behave when I mounted him for the first time, for I was determined now to retrain him before the end of the summer holidays. Of course I had never met Arabella who was at boarding school, but I imagined she couldn't be annoyed because any normal person would welcome any action that would save so friendly and beautiful a pony from an early and unnecessary death. I knew that Cassidy was lonely because he welcomed me eagerly every morning with a soft whinny, pricked ears and shining eyes. Sometimes I saw a boy in the theatrical people's house watching me from a window, and occasionally I heard their dog barking. Otherwise I was very much alone while Patsy ran her shop or went to auctions to buy antiques, with the pony my special and only friend.

When Friday evening came I put on my jodhpurs, which were getting a little small for me, and a denim shirt, and pushed my hair into a horrible net, which Patsy had bought for me at the village post office, and walked down to the riding school.

Miss Kirk was in the yard with the girl with the dark fringe, and six or seven children.

"Oh, you must be Miss Cooper's niece," said Miss Kirk, looking me up and down with a pair of sharp blue eyes under thickish brows.

"God-daughter," I replied, tactlessly because grown-ups don't always like to be corrected by younger people. "I'm staying with her while my mother is in Russia."

"Haven't you got a father?" asked Miss Kirk with a laugh.

"Well, yes, in Russia, that's the point. My mother's gone to see him."

"It sounds very complicated. Well now, you have the Exmoor over there, named Mousie, after the character in the book. She's a bit small for you but very safe. She won't take-off or anything. I understand you've never had a lesson in your life." She gave another funny little laugh as though this made me quite out of the ordinary.

"Yes, but a farmer friend taught me how to sit and hold the reins. I know that I must keep my heels and hands down, and that sort of thing."

"Farmers are not known for their good horsemanship," said Miss Kirk, rather crushingly. "Pippa, help this little Russian up will you?"

A young girl with fair hair, bright cheeks and a jaw like a sheep's mouth came out of the tack room and untied an Exmoor mare with a mealy nose, wide forehead and rather straight shoulder.

"I'm only half Russian and I came over as a baby," I said.

"That still makes you an *émigrée*," said the girl. "Have you got a whip?"

"No."

"I'll see if I can borrow one for you. Mousie's not exactly the liveliest pony in the school."

After the fell ponies my mount felt narrow and small, and her ears seemed uncomfortably near my face. She needed kicking to get her started.

Pippa mounted the grey I had admired on my first visit and led the ride round the school. There were seven of us. We spent the first five minutes walking with Miss Kirk commenting on the way we sat, held the reins or handled our ponies.

"For future reference, I like my pupils in collars and ties, Katie," she said. "A sloppily dressed child is usually an untidy rider, too. Right, prepare to trot . . . t. .r. .o. .t."

I didn't feel at all out of practice and it was lovely just to be on a pony again, but I disliked Miss Kirk, as she stood in the middle of the school hitting her boots with a riding whip and criticizing us. I thought that if only my mother had been here we would have had such fun discussing her afterwards, for my mother, hating pomposity or self importance, was marvellous at making fun of people. Presently we each cantered round in turn. I had difficulty in getting Mousie to start on the right leg, but succeeded the third time after having the diagonal aids painstakingly explained to me.

Then Miss Kirk arranged some cavaletti jumps for us, and I rode Mousie at them as I had ridden Destiny and Captain, and she refused.

"No push! Put some guts into it," said Miss Kirk. "Come on, kick! Are you frightened?"

"No, of course not," I said, feeling very hot and cross. "I've jumped three feet."

"Well, come on, ride then. Show us what you can do. Don't just sit there," retorted Miss Kirk.

"Use the stick, behind your leg," whispered a small girl on a sweet little pony called Smudgey.

Destiny and Captain had needed holding back until the last three strides, when they were put at a jump, and I had fallen off several times before I had learned to manage them. I had never had to use a stick before. But this time I whacked Mousie and kicked her with both my legs, and she jumped the three cavaletti.

"That's right. Let her see who's Boss," said Miss Kirk. "Next please. Come on Jenny, what are you standing about for with your mouth open? Wake up!"

At the end of the lesson we had a walk, trot and canter race, and played musical blocks, and I was last but one in each competition. Then we unsaddled and unbridled our ponies, gave them a drink and turned them out in a field.

"Do you want another lesson soon?" asked Miss Kirk, looking in the book. "There's plenty of room for improvement, but you have promise."

"I don't know," I said. "You see my mother's in Russia."

"Yes, I've gathered that," said Miss Kirk. "Well, that will be two pounds fifty please."

I handed her my lovely crisp five-pound note.

"I suppose you don't need any help in the stables. I'm good at mucking out," I ventured.

"Well, you haven't got the experience have you? Let's face it. We should have to teach you and we haven't the time to spare just now, dear," Miss Kirk gave me a sort of half smile, as she handed me two dirty, crumpled pound notes and a fifty pence piece. "Will your mother be all right in Russia? She's British by birth I suppose."

"Oh yes, she's been before. She knows her way around, and my father's there. He's a pretty powerful sort of person I should think."

"Is he a communist?"

"I don't know, I suppose so. He's high up in some factory, I believe. It's all connected with timber."

"He must be a trade unionist. I wouldn't be in her shoes," said tactless Miss Kirk. "Well, I hope we shall see you for another lesson some time."

"Yes, that's right," I said. "Thank you very much."

I tore off the beastly hairnet as I walked down the drive and threw it in the hedge, and kicked a stone furiously before me.

Patsy was already home when I arrived back at the lodge.

"All right? Had a good time, fixed everything up?" she smiled at me brightly, wanting to believe that I was settling down with a sort of unpaid job at the riding school.

"Yes, fine thank you."

"Well done, old thing," she patted me on the back. "We should be hearing from your mother any day now."

"Miss Kirk said she wouldn't like to be in her shoes," I said, filling a cup with water.

"No, nor would I, but your mother always springs back again. Nothing keeps her down for long. By the way, do you know what's happened to the rope that hangs in the garage? I need it to tie a table to the roof of the car."

"Oh, you mean the halter?" I said.

"No, a rope. I haven't got a halter, Katie, love."

"I'll fetch it, hang on," I said.

"Yes, do. I need it for my job." Patsy had an edge to her voice, so I ran.

I found the halter hanging on the iron railings and tried

to undo the knots and turn it into a rope again. I tugged and pulled and sweated and hurt the remains of my bitten nails without success, and then Patsy came out to see where I was.

"I'm dreadfully sorry. I used it as a halter, I couldn't find anything else," I said.

"Which isn't surprising since I'm an antique dealer and not a saddler, farmer or horse dealer," said Patsy cryptically. "Bring it in and we'll struggle with the knots after we've eaten. I'm grilling chops and they won't wait."

It was ten o'clock before we managed to turn the halter into a rope again, and then Patsy decided we had better refresh ourselves with bitter lemon and ice, and the bottle opener wasn't there. I fetched it and the clothes brush and confessed that I had helped myself to them, and I washed them both in soapy water and disinfectant in the kitchen sink.

"You are an egotist," said Patsy crossly, "you think of no one but yourself."

"I think of the pony. Perhaps it's because I'm a Russian *émigrée*, perhaps that makes me different from other people. Perhaps my grandfather was a Cossack," I replied splashing lather around.

"Are you a Russian *émigrée*? Yes, I suppose you are. I never thought of that. Of course you were born in Russia, weren't you? That's why your mother couldn't take you with her. They might have kept you."

"She didn't tell me that. I thought she just couldn't afford the air fare."

"Maybe, but I expect your father would have liked to see you."

"Will he come back with her?" I asked, glad to have taken Patsy's mind off the clothes brush, rope and bottle opener.

"I shouldn't think so. She isn't happy in Russia and he can't bear to leave, or perhaps he isn't allowed to."

"Well, if she can't bear it why has she gone back?"

"To sort things out I suppose," said Patsy darkly. "But I only mean she can't bear to live there permanently. Your mother likes to speak spontaneously, without thinking, and that doesn't do in the Soviet Union. You can't say out loud, "I hate the President," without risking imprisonment."

So the evening ended on a friendly note, but I hadn't the courage to explain that Miss Kirk didn't want my help, since Patsy had convinced herself that from now on I would be happily occupied at the riding school.

"I've left some sliced bread, corned beef and butter ready for you to make sandwiches to take tomorrow," she called last thing, as I crawled under the duvet on my divan bed. My window overlooked the honeysuckle and a corner of the field, and the sound of Cassidy cropping the grass was like music in my ears. At least he cares for me, I thought.

CHAPTER FOUR

I MEET MATTHEW

The next day it was raining and I woke up feeling miserable with the thought that I had nowhere to go and nothing to do. Patsy had said I could read any of her books but, although I was thirteen, they were all too difficult for me, and when I went downstairs she had already gone, leaving a note which I couldn't understand. Felix had disappeared and Cassidy was standing under a tree with his back to the wind.

I made myself toast and found butter and marmalade, and tried to drown my sorrows in coffee. I fetched the radio and twiddled the dial, but could find no programme that interested me. My solace at our many homes had been television, which had taught me far more than any teachers in the schools I had attended. Now I was lost without it.

After a time I started wandering about the house looking at Patsy's knick-knacks. There were lots of little porcelain figures and rather pretty enamelled boxes in lovely dark colours, a few horse brasses, and a small collection of pistols. I had just picked up a blunderbuss when the telephone rang with sudden and shrill urgency. Dropping the blunderbuss guiltily I dashed across and snatched up the receiver, glad of anything that would break the monotony. After the operator had checked my number she told me to hold on for a call from Moscow and within moments Mummy was at the other end, talking quite clearly.

"Katerina, darling. How are you?"

"Fine, thank you, just fine," I said.

"Have you settled in all right? Is Patsy there?"

I said I had fitted in beautifully and that Patsy was at her shop.

"There's a nice cat here called Felix and a pony called Cassidy who is to be shot in the autumn."

"Have you made friends at the riding school?"

"No, not yet," I said.

"It takes time sometimes," my mother said. "But don't give up hope. I had a rotten journey with two hours' delay in Helsinki, but everything's fine now. Here's your father, wanting to speak to you. Hold on."

A foreign voice with a strong accent took over and said: "Katerina, it's your Daddy, your Papa. Do you remember me? No, of course you don't. Well, I give you my love, and be a good girl, do you hear? Be a good girl and work hard at school, always work, study."

For a moment I was horribly tongue-tied, and then the foreign voice said: "Are you there, do you hear me, Katerina, my little daughter?"

And I said: "Yes, I do, but I don't know what to say. I don't remember you. Is it hot there? Is the sun shining? Is Mummy all right?"

And the foreign voice said: "Yes, everything's fine," and then there was a click and the sound of someone talking in Russian and that was all. Feeling rather flat, I put down the receiver and cuddled Felix who had just come into the room. Then I looked out of the window and saw the rain had stopped and that Cassidy was at the railing waiting for my morning visit. I cut a slice of bread off the loaf and took it over to him.

"I've been speaking to a Russian," I told him, because there was no one else to tell, "and to my mother and everything's fine, but I've no halter for you or grooming tools or anything."

Then I remembered that I still had two crumpled pound notes, so I went to the post office and asked where the nearest saddler was, and the woman behind the counter said Solihull, which was three miles away. So I put on an old anorak over my denims and walked to Solihull. I found the saddler's shop and bought a jute halter, a dandy brush and a hoof pick, and that was the end of everything but tuppence.

The walk back seemed very long, and it started to rain again, and by the time I was home my jeans were soaked. I took them off and hung them on a radiator and put on my jodhpurs, then I made myself a sandwich and another cup of coffee, and then it was three o'clock.

The rain had eased so I went into the field and led Cassidy up and down, and saw the dark-haired boy watching me from the window in the theatrical people's house. After a bit I waved, but he didn't wave back. He was wearing a hugger jacket and his hair was cut in a fringe, and his nose was overlarge.

Cassidy was very sweet and did everything I asked him to do, and afterwards he nuzzled my jodhpurs and sniffed my hair. I wondered whether the boy saw how good he was, and whether the boy wondered who I was and why I wasn't at school like everyone else. Then I remembered that it was Saturday, and I realized that it was five days since my mother had left for Russia.

Patsy came home at a quarter to six and said she was going to take me to see a film, and had I had a good day?

I said, yes, fine thank you, and she said it was so fortunate that I liked ponies and that there was a riding school in the village and that everything was working out so well, and that she must give Miss Kirk the shop telephone number in case I fell off or anything.

"Or rather you can do that, can't you? Copy it down on a card and then if you sprain your wrist or anything she can give me a call. I'm only twenty minutes away by car."

The film was set in the last war and made Patsy very nostalgic, and afterwards we sat talking far into the night. She told me that she had been a Wren in the war, attached to the Royal Navy, and she talked a little about her husband, who had been killed a week before the end of hostilities. On my way to bed I told her about the call from Moscow and she said: "You are a funny old thing, keeping that bit of news up your sleeve for so long."

I said: "It seemed very odd talking to a father I've never seen. I was pretty dumb. I couldn't think of anything to say." Patsy asked whether my mother had given me an address to which I could write and, when I said no, Patsy said that was just like my mother; she hadn't changed a bit. Then I asked how Patsy had come to meet my mother and she said through an advertisement in a national newspaper, when Patsy had been looking for an assistant for her antique shop.

"She worked for you?"

"Yes, and farmed you out with a lovely fat woman called Mrs. Smithers, whom you adored."

"Why did she leave?"

"Your mother always leaves," said Patsy. "She never stays in a job for more than two years. She's one of the world's wanderers. She's a nomad, Katie. You are a gypsy child. I am surprised you've got educated at all."

"Her parents?" I asked. "My Grannie and Grandad? I've never quite understood about them."

"They were killed in a car crash," said Patsy. "That's why your mother wanders, she's always looking for the home and security she lost when she was small. Now your face is pale with fatigue. Off to bed and I'll bring you some cocoa. How about that?"

So another day ended; and the next was Sunday. I spent most of it helping Patsy to clean some old stained glass she had bought for next to nothing from a demolition man. Afterwards she gave me a pound. "My goodness, you've earned it for sheer elbow grease," she said. Then I began to feel better, because I knew that we were beginning to adjust to each other.

On Monday I put my arm across Cassidy's back and all but mounted him, then I vaulted halfway on and lay across him, talking all the time, and he stood quite still, listening with his ears back.

"You like me now, don't you? We are friends, aren't we? We trust one another." I slipped down and picked up his hoofs one by one and crawled under him. I looked into

31

his mouth, and lifted his tail and he didn't turn a hair. Then I fetched Felix and put him on Cassidy's back and the pony stood like a rock, quiet and unconcerned. "I won't let you be shot. There's been a dreadful mistake." I said. "You shan't die. I've made it my mission in life to save you."

The sun was shining and all at once I felt very cheerful, and I began to sing one of Abba's songs. Then I thought: why postpone the great act any longer? He'll never be quieter than this, and I vaulted halfway on him again, so that I lay on my stomach on his back. Then slowly and quietly I slid my body an inch or two further, so that I could slip my right leg over. I twisted from the hips and waist, sat up and for one triumphant second was about to ride him. I moved to pat him on the neck, and in the same instant all hell seemed to break loose. His back arched, his body twisted, his head and neck disappeared, and then I flew into the air like a ball, up, up and then down, with the earth rising to meet me. There was a horrible thud as I hit the ground, stars danced before my eyes, followed by a moment's blackness. Then I opened my eyes and the earth stopped heaving, and slowly I sat up. I turned my head and saw Cassidy racing backwards across the field pulling an iron railing after him. His eyes were large and terrified and his nostrils dilated.

"Whoa," I said. "Whoa."

This time my training paid off for he stopped and stood stock still trembling from head to foot. Talking all the time, I stole up to him and managed to slip off the halter so that he was free of the railing, then feeling incredibly groggy I leaned against him. He nuzzled me searching my pockets for food, and I swear his dark eyes were full of trust and affection. There was no evil, no wickedness in them.

"Why?" I asked, weakly.

And another voice said: "Are you all right? It was the devil of a fall!"

There was the son of the theatrical people, the boy at the window, standing before me, smiling diffidently. "You had better come in and sit down. You may be concussed. Come on!"

He took my arm and led me across the field to his parents' brick and flint cottage, which smelt of roses and spice and herbs. He sat me down on a stripped pine chair in the cheerful white kitchen.

"That pony's vicious," he said. "Didn't Miss Cooper warn you?"

"Oh yes, but I thought I had cured him, and I made several idiotic mistakes. I tied him straight to the railings instead of to a loop of baling string which would have broken when he pulled back suddenly. And I had no one standing at his head. I'm mad, sometimes I think I'm mad. I do such stupid things and hate myself afterwards."

"Oh, we all do that," said the boy. "Do you ache anywhere? Did you hit your head? You didn't even put on a crash cap."

"Luckily I think I landed on my bottom," I said. "I must have turned round in the air. I feel sore, but that's all. I can remember everything, so I'm not concussed."

"Do your arms and legs work? Arabella had quite a nasty break—she was a week in hospital—and now she's full of pins."

I banged my arms up and down, turned my head this way and that, and said, "Yes, perhaps I'm fat enough to bounce."

"I'll make you a cup of tea then, that's good for shock, sugared tea. I'm Matthew, by the way, Matthew Trumpington. Now don't make a funny joke about Enid Blyton, I can't bear it."

"I'm Katerina Turgenieff, Katie to most people."

"That sounds very foreign, Russian?"

"Yes, I'm an *émigrée*. I came over when I was a few months old."

"That's great. I've never met a Russian before. Can you speak the language and read that terrifying alphabet?"

"No, but my mother can. She's English, by the way. She went over to study there or something, and fell in love with my father. She's a very unusual person."

"And you were the result?" said Matthew laughing, as he put on the kettle.

"Now she's in Moscow with my father, and I'm here until she gets back."

"Sorting things out I suppose," said Matthew. "Are they married?"

"Of course they are married," I said hotly. "It's just that my mother didn't like living in the Soviet Union."

"Which isn't surprising. It's very different from here," said Matthew, taking down a wooden tea caddy. "Is she trying to arrange for him to come over here?"

"I don't think so. I don't think he would be allowed to come, and she's always said he loved his motherland too well to leave it. That's what she tells anyone who asks silly questions."

I wanted suddenly to tell him everything.

"Perhaps they'll get a divorce then."

"Oh, I shouldn't think so."

Just then a great golden chow came into the room, grandly, like a lion.

"This is Tao," said Matthew, "my friend and guard."

The dog looked at me, then came across and licked my hand with a purple tongue.

"She doesn't do that to everyone. It means she likes you," said Matthew, spooning tea into a blue-and-white pot.

There was a moment's silence then I said: "I know it's none of my business and I've got an awful cheek, but I don't want Cassidy to be shot. I'm quite sure he doesn't mean to hurt people. He's just got on the wrong wavelength. He thinks bucking is the right thing to do. I'm convinced of that."

"But he's done so much damage. His reputation is finished. It's better that he goes for dog meat. You must be realistic," said Matthew pouring milk into blue-and-white mugs. "I mean animals have to earn their keep one way or another. I think Arabella's parents are quite generous to let him live in that field until autumn. He's no use to them. He's a killer."

"But he's beautiful. He's friendly, alive, with a beating heart and a sleek coat and gleaming eyes. He's a joy to look at. Don't you understand?"

"Oh, you're impossibly romantic," said Matthew laughing. "Here, drink your tea and come down to earth." He smiled at me.

34

We sat in silence for another moment, either side of a pine table, sipping the warm, sweet tea. Matthew's eyes were dark brown, touched with green, below thick arched brows that almost met above his rather large nose. He had a pleasant, slightly apologetic grin that split his face which was well rounded with a fresh complexion. He looked good natured and straightforward. I supposed that my mother would have described him as open-faced.

"Do you live alone?" I asked, at last.

"Not really. It all depends on when and where my parents are working. Just now my mother has a television show on three evenings a week, her own show, rather like Esther Rantzen's, and my father is making a film in Morocco. Mother, well we call each other by first names in this house—Penelope—will be home this evening and out tomorrow night. I'm fourteen and a half, so it's perfectly legal to leave me alone all night, and she always rings me several times every twenty-four hours, and Tao guards me, and Mrs. Carter comes in to clean every morning."

"Don't you go to school?" I asked.

"Oh yes, you've seen me around, because I've had a touch of glandular fever, but I'm just about through that. I'm to have another blood test next week, when I'm sure I shall be in the clear. I have another companion, too. Hang on, I'll bring him down for you to see."

I watched Matthew as he left the room: tall and thin, but with wide shoulders and a long stride. I wondered whether he would let me watch his television set. Then I heard him running up the stairs, his voice calling: "Rex, Rex, come on, here, Rex." And, a moment or two later, he was back with a rat on his shoulder.

"This is Rex, a king among rodents," he said, with a grin. "A white Norwegian hooded rat, very intelligent."

Rex peeped down at me, his little nostrils working as he picked up my scent; he eyes bright as boot buttons. His head and neck were mousey brown and the rest of him glistening white. His long pale tail curled round Matthew's neck. Every now and then he looked enquiringly at his master, then gently licked his cheek with a little pink tongue.

"Of course, I'm terrified that Mrs. Cooper's cat will get in," said Matthew.

"He's sweet," I said, getting up to stroke the sleek brown fur. "What does he eat?"

"Anything really, but he likes sunflower seeds and meat. And a bit of lettuce, too. He has what I have, really."

"He's quite fat."

"Too fat, aren't you, Rexy," said Matthew, fondly stroking the little rat's face.

"He looks so affectionate," I said.

"I'm glad you like him," said Matthew. "I hate girls who scream and shriek when they see toads or mice or rats. It seems so uncivilized."

"Do you have colour television?" I asked.

"You mean for the wildlife programmes?"

"No, generally. We've always had black and white."

"Yes, we do. Do you want to watch it?"

"Oh yes, please." I said. "Patsy hasn't a set at all. She says she never needed a stimulus like that when she was a child. Now I'm missing all my favourite programmes."

"Well, come here whenever you like," said Matthew. "Would you like to hold Rex? No, it's all right, Tao likes him, thinks of him as a puppy. They're friends."

He gave me the warm little body and the rat ran up my arm and settled on my shoulder.

CHAPTER FIVE

I MEET A RAT

The next day a postcard arrived from my mother. It was of the Kremlin, in Moscow. It had taken four days to come, and I couldn't decipher the handwriting. Patsy had already left for the shop, leaving a message I couldn't understand, so I made myself toast and switched on the radio. As usual my Godmother had left me something for lunch; this time a brown, sliced, wholemeal loaf, cheese and cress, and a banana. She had truly convinced herself without any help from me that I would be spending every day at the riding school, and I could not bring myself to enlighten her with the truth. I told myself that this delusion gave her peace of mind and enabled her to work all day thinking that I was in safe hands, watched over by the brusque but efficient Miss Kirk.

It was a wild, cloudy day with the wind tossing all the young diseased apples from the trees, and turning the ripening corn on the other side of the road into rippling waves of cream.

I went outside and talked to Cassidy for a while. He seemed uneasy, probably because of the wind which lifted his mane and blew his thick black tail between his legs. Felix came and sat with us, purring and looking up at me with incredibly green eyes. He had a beautiful white waist-coat, a wide face and exceptionally pointed ears which, Patsy said, showed that he had Abyssinian blood in him. He was one of the most handsome cats I had ever seen, lithe and sinuous, tiger striped, and with the air of an aristocrat. But he was lazy; he never hunted and I wondered whether he would really bother to kill Rex if he came across him.

I had asked Patsy her opinion on the Trumpingtons, while we ate supper the night before, and she had said that they were like all theatrical people: affected, smartly dressed, charming, unreliable and to some extent irres-ponsible. "They are very fond of Matthew, of course," she had said, "but they put their careers first. They are ambitious and self-centred. You have to be to succeed in the theatre world."

"Would they be what my mother calls shallow?" I asked.

"Well, not exactly," Patsy had replied, after a thoughtful pause. "Because they see drama as an art to which they are dedicated. I think your mother might find them false."

"And the boy?"

"Oh, he seems nice enough, a bit of a loner, which isn't surprising. If he were my son I'd want to toughen him up a bit. Get him into the rugger field or out for cross-country runs. But then I'm old fashioned. In my day fresh air and exercise were thought important. I enjoyed hockey and netball. He's spoilt, too, has everything he wants, a racing cycle he never rides, a violin he gave up playing, stereo, a tape recorder and heaven knows what else. But, of course, when I was a teenager we were on the brink of war and after that there was rationing. We couldn't be obsessed with gear and clothes and all that rubbish. We had to think about fighting for our country. Why, I was an expert sock-darner by the time I was thirteen, and busy knitting blankets for refugees. We couldn't be self-centred, not in those days. It just wasn't done and, by golly, we worked. No time for things like glandular fever then!"

Patsy undoubtedly believed in toil; she couldn't bear to see me "mooning about" as she called it. In the evenings she set me cleaning furniture, and taught me how to cane chairs. "If you're not going to read and enlarge your mind you might as well work," she said.

Meanwhile I worried about Cassidy. I was obsessed with the idea that he had been taught to buck, and the next afternoon I went to discuss my theory with Matthew.

"You see, no one has really considered his mind," I said. "He's been through some conditioning process."

"He was sold as unbroken," Matthew reminded me. "Arabella showed me his entry in the catalogue of the sale."

"Are bucking broncos used in films?"

"Not over here, I think. In America for Westerns, yes, but Cassidy's a bit small for that role. You are not suggesting he's an ex-film-star I hope; that would be ridiculous."

"No, no. Can I see Rex?" I asked, wanting to change the subject in case I was being silly. Then Matthew said good naturedly: "Of course, any time," and took me upstairs to his room, which was enormous and raftered. The floor was covered in expensive and rather beautifully patterned linoleum. His bed was in one corner with a goatskin rug thrown over it, and Rex was curled up asleep in a square cardboard box which had once held a football.

"I'm afraid I haven't cleaned the room lately, apart from sweeping up after Rex," confessed Matthew. "Mrs. Carter won't touch it because she's frightened of rats. But I don't think dust matters much, do you?"

"No, and cobwebs are useful, because they stop bleeding," I said. "A farmer friend in the fells told me that."

"And also because they catch flies, and you can see the spider at work," added Matthew.

Rex woke up then and made little squeaky noises to welcome us. Matthew gave him sunflower seeds, which he ate like a squirrel, sitting on his haunches and holding them in his little hands (they were far too delicate to be called paws) and peeling off the outside husk with his teeth. Then he licked his palms and wiped his fur with them, and Tao came in and tried to wash him, with her tongue.

"She wants to be a mother," said Matthew.

I sat down on the floor and buried my face in the dog's ruff, liking the feel of the fur against my face. There were two tanks of fish in Matthew's room, and three terrapins, and lots of pictures of wild animals, stuck on the wall with *Bluetak.*

Presently I got up and wandered round looking at them. "I can lend you a book about all the threatened species if you're interested," offered Matthew. He took a thick, lavishly illustrated volume down from the shelf and handed it to me. "Penelope's on a committee which has been set up to discourage females from wearing real furs."

I looked at the book but most of the words danced in a hopeless blur before my eyes.

"Oh, and there's something in the paper this morning about poachers killing hundreds of African elephants for their ivory tusks. Hold on, I'll get it."

He went way and came back with a newspaper.

"Read it, page four. Look, horrible isn't it? Aren't people foul?"

I found the place, marked by a photograph, and ran my eyes over the print.

"You're not reading it," said Matthew accusingly.

"Yes, I am. Can I watch your telly? There's a programme at a quarter to four I like. Honestly I feel starved without a set at Patsy's."

Matthew pointed to a nineteen-inch model in his bedroom, placed so that he could view it from his bed.

"In here or downstairs?"

"Oh, in colour, please; that will be a novelty." I put down the paper and started to bite my nails.

We went down to the sitting-room with Rex riding on Matthew's shoulder and Tao panting at our heels.

The furniture here was modern, deep chairs and a sofa, covered in mustard-coloured corduroy, and a round pine table.

When my programme ended we made tea in the kitchen and ate a packet of wholemeal chocolate biscuits, which were in the lavishly stocked pine corner cupboard. Food always seemed to be plentiful in this kitchen; the deep freeze, the cupboards and refrigerator stacked high with delicious provisions of all kinds. It was all very different from my mother's frugal way of life, broken now and then when a little good fortune came her way to be celebrated by a dinner at some exotic restaurant. Everything here was also pleasantly light and cheerful in contrast with Patsy's lodge, where the rather gloomy atmosphere was increased by dark antique furniture.

"My mother inherited this place," Matthew now explained. "It would be much easier in many ways if we all lived in London, but she can't bear to leave. She says the countryside is healthier for children, i.e., *me*. She's going to retire here with Meredith when their acting days are over."

"Meredith?"

"My father."

"Oh yes, of course," I said, telling myself not to be a fool, to remember that television and film people are not conventional.

"We are very trendy; we move with the times," said Matthew, with one of his little self-mocking, half apologetic smiles. "No old-fashioned Mummy and Daddy in this place!"

I asked whether he was going to be an actor, looking at his face and trying to judge its possibilities for the screen, too.

"No way," he exploded. "I want to be a vet."

I said that he must be doing well at school and he answered that he wasn't; his chemistry and physics were frightful.

I went back to Patsy's place at six o'clock, put the halter on Cassidy and groomed him. His sweetness and good temper made me feel very sad. "There's no reason why you shouldn't look your best," I said, remembering how a little frizzy-haired school teacher had told me that Mary Queen of Scots had made up her face and dressed beautifully for her execution. I supposed, rather miserably, that Cassidy would be absolutely dead before he was fed to hounds.

I was busy brushing out his tail when I heard footsteps in the grass and, turning, saw a slim, fair girl approaching, a frown creasing her narrow well-bred forehead.

As she walked, her mouth opened wide; she gesticulated. "What do you think you are doing, grooming my pony?" she bellowed in a voice which did not match her sophisticated appearance. "You are trespassing!"

I waited until she was nearer before answering, because I wanted to collect my wits and quieten my pounding heart.

"He's lonely," I said at last. "And I'm grooming him, because he's sad and bored, and if he's to die I might as well make his last weeks cheerful." I gave a gulp because, suddenly, I was full of pity for both Cassidy and, less understandably, myself.

"But where do you come from? Who are you?"

She spoke now as though she owned the village and I was some interloper who had dared to stray inside the magic boundary without her knowledge or permission.

"I come from Russia," I replied dramatically, dividing strands of Cassidy's jet-black tail.

"Oh, big joke! Come on, let's have the truth. Out with it!" demanded the girl with a bullying edge to her voice. "Who are you and why are you in Daddy's field? This is private property, you know."

"I'm staying with Patsy Cooper. She's my Godmother," I replied, brushing furiously, red in the face because I had not been believed.

"Don't!" cried Arabella. "You are breaking the hairs. Don't you know that tails should never be groomed with dandy brushes?"

"I couldn't afford a body brush as well," I said, looking up again at last.

"Oh," said Arabella, very taken aback. "Do you mean

to say you bought these grooming tools just to groom my pony? You must be nuts!"

"I'm not like you," I said, as though that were a relief to me. "I'm a Russian *émigrée*, so I couldn't be, could I? But at least I don't go round having beautiful ponies killed."

"You don't look Russian," remarked Arabella, leaning against the fence with all the elegance of a pale saluki dog.

"And you don't look English," I retorted stoutly. "You look Swedish," and I stared pointedly at her golden skin and long flaxen hair which fell elegantly to her shoulders.

Mollified, it seemed, she said: "Oh well, if you want to groom Cassidy you can. It can't do any harm, and if it gives you pleasure," she gesticulated vaguely: "So long as you don't try riding him. He's dangerous, you see, and he's mine, so if anything happened to you, it would be my fault, or could be considered so. He could kill you. No, I am serious. Please don't ride him, but pet and groom him if you must make him into a live doll!"

"I've been told about the bucking," I said. "Animals can't be dolls."

"Well, look," said Arabella, rolling back a sleeve of her pink-and-white striped shirt to reveal a scar which stretched an inch or more above and below the elbow. "I'm not just being dog-in-the-manger."

"Yes, I know, you're pinned. Bad luck!" I tried to forget the doll jibe, although it cut deep.

"Who told you?"

"Patsy and Matthew."

"That weird boy who lives in that cottage with a chow and a rat?" She laughed, a cool little derisive sound, which made anger rise up in me again, like sap in a tree when spring comes suddenly and late.

"Well, I mean, a rat! It's a bit off, isn't it?" she screwed up her nose as though she had met a bad smell. "And he lets that tail wrap around his neck. It's peculiar. People say he doesn't go to school any more and is withdrawing into himself. Oh well, it's none of my business."

"No, and he's nice," I said. "He's had glandular fever."

"His parents are famous, of course," mused Arabella. "You've probably seen his mother on that trashy telly programme. Pure rubbish of course, but madly popular."

"I like it, as it happens," I said.

"Fair enough," replied Arabella. "But I don't. How long are you here for?" She felt in a pocket almost as though she was looking for a cigarette, then ran a slender hand through her hair. It seemed unfair to me then that she should be both rich and beautiful and, in addition, a champion rider.

"I don't know. It depends when my mother comes back from Russia."

"So you really are from the Soviet Union," Arabella sounded incredulous.

"Half Russian, born there, brought up here." As I spoke, I turned Cassidy loose. He walked away a few strides, turned round three times and then lay down and rolled.

"All your good work undone," said Arabella, with a merry laugh. "Yes, do go ahead and groom him if it gives you pleasure."

"He likes listening to the radio," I said. "He's very intelligent."

"Yes, most ponies enjoy music," she agreed. "Look, Why don't you take riding lessons from Miss Kirk. She's a fierce old thing, but a first-rate teacher. She started me off."

"Yes, I might," I said. And then I saw Patsy in the garden, calling. "I must be off," I added. "My Godmother is back and I must help to get supper. Do try to think of something. You can't kill Cassidy."

"We have, and failed. The death sentence stands," the girl answered moving away from the fence. "I'm sorry." I looked at her then, full in the face, for the first time, trying to change her mind by what I imagined might be a withering glance. She was all I wanted to be! Slim, tall with that fine straight nose and almond-shaped, hazel flecked eyes in a golden face touched by the faintest pink on the cheeks that curved gently like pears. She made me feel clumsy and inadequate. In comparison, my cheeks were like apples and my eyes too bold and blue. My hair, parted in the middle, was dark brown like my mother's but inclined to lankness. My figure, although slim, was sturdy rather than elegant, and although I had inherited my mother's narrow hands they could not compete with the smooth slenderness of Arabella's.

"Coming," I shouted to Patsy, as I started to walk back across the lawn, carrying the halter and dandy brush.

"Didn't you get my message?"

She was in the kitchen doorway; her eyes ablaze, her greying black hair awry; her mouth twisted into a humourless smile.

"What message?" Her anger seemed to envelop me. My heart began to hammer again. What had I done this time? I searched my conscience without positive result.

"Oh, don't say you didn't see it! Oh Katie, that is really too much! I lodged it up against the bread bin, as large as life. You must have moved it before you made your toast."

"Oh, that bit of cardboard?"

"You admit you saw it?"

"I'm terribly sorry. I put it to one side." Feeling suddenly very tired, I started to bite my nails.

"Then, why didn't you read it?" Her eyes began to bulge now, hard and round as dark berries behind her glasses. Her anger seemed a separate force, hovering between us.

"I don't know."

"You must know," she cried. "You are lying. I know you're lying. I have been kind to you. Why do you let me down? Your face is turning red. You have a guilty conscience!"

I tried one more possible loophole to escape telling the truth.

"I forgot," I whispered. "I'm sorry, Patsy. Was it very important?"

"I don't believe you. What am I to do? The steak had to be out of the deep freeze by two o'clock. It's hard as rock. I have an important American customer coming at eight o'clock. This is a disaster for me. Can't you see that, you silly child? I am a business woman. I have to earn my living. I need the good will of these people!"

"But I don't even know where the deep freeze is," I shouted.

"But I wrote that on the message. It's in the garage. I said so."

"I'm sorry," I repeated. "Dreadfully sorry."

"Well, what do you expect me to do?" asked Patsy. "If it was Friday, shops would be open late, but on a Tuesday everything's shut by now. You've wrecked my evening, you horrid child!"

"A restaurant," I suggested timidly.

"I can't take a rich American to a restaurant. He would end up by paying. I couldn't do that. It would be embarrassing."

"Matthew," I said, blinking hard.

"What about Matthew?"

"His family have a deep freeze. I've seen it."

"And why have you been with that boy?" Her voice seemed to suggest all sorts of awful happenings and I realized that, in this mood, she would see the black side of everything.

"Watching telly," I replied as calmly as I could.

"Oh, I see, but his deep freeze food will be frozen too, silly! Oh, why did you have to let me down now of all times? I've had a terrible day. I sold someone a Georgian table a few weeks ago, which an expert at the Victoria and Albert Museum has suggested is a fake. And now this! I can feel a migraine coming on."

To my horror I saw that Patsy was also blinking back tears.

"I'm sorry, but I'm sure Matthew can help. His cupboards are full of things. Just wait!"

I wanted to escape. I ran like a beaten dog to a place of refuge.

Tao barked as I knocked at the door and then Matthew came.

"Want to watch television?" he asked with his broad, good-natured grin, which, after Patsy's torrent of words, was like cool water after the heat of a furnace.

"No, I'm in trouble." I told him about the steak.

"Oh, what a fuss about a bit of food!" he said. "I'm sure we can find something. Penelope doesn't often cook but when she does, the result is brilliant."

He opened a cupboard door. "Caviar (that should warm your little Russian heart) or canned prawns or chicken in

45

aspic, grouse in wine sauce, ravioli, loganberries, raspberries, vichyssoise soup."

"The grouse, please," I said after a long pause.

"Here you are then, and take the prawns for starters."

I said that I had seen éclairs and cheese in her basket so I thought she would now be all right. "Thank you very much."

"Any time," he said.

I ran back to find Patsy looking calmer as she peeled potatoes.

"Any luck?" she managed a smile.

"Here." I handed her the tins.

"Good heavens, that looks grand. Fortnum and Masons, how nice! How much?"

"He didn't say. I never thought." I began to bite my nails again. "Perhaps you can sort that out with his mother later."

"I'm sorry I blew my top. I shouldn't have shouted at you. I do apologize," Patsy said, putting potatoes into a saucepan.

"It's all right," I said, feeling horribly embarrassed.

"Let's both forget it," suggested Patsy. "Now be an angel. I need your help. He will be here in forty minutes and I've got to change. Take down that cook book and look up prawns for me, will you? Find a recipe, which will do for starters, and read it out. Hurry child, and do stop biting those nails, there'll be nothing left soon!"

"I can't," I said.

"You can't. What do you mean?"

"I can't read," I said, and then I ran from the room with my eyes smarting and my throat suddenly as rough and dry as sandpaper.

CHAPTER SIX

I ASK MATTHEW'S ADVICE

I cried in bed that night. I cried because I couldn't read and had let Patsy down, and because Cassidy was going to die and I didn't know how to save him.

Outside, rain dripped from the honeysuckle and Felix mewed at the garden door, and the sound of a disc on Matthew's stereo beat the air like a tribal dance.

Patsy hadn't been unkind. She had said I was remarkably intelligent for someone who couldn't read. She had asked me how I had learned so much. And I had told her from radio and television, and she had said no wonder I had got lost on the train if I couldn't read the names of stations; my mother had, of course, hinted at the situation but never spelt it out. I had wanted then to ask her to read the Kremlin postcard to me, but decided she was too busy preparing for her American customer. He turned out to be a fat man with a jolly face and a cigar sticking out of a corner of his mouth, just like an American character on television.

I didn't have any grouse because it looked rather small and, as Patsy said, Americans liked big helpings. I heated up baked beans instead and, after that, I had gone to bed feeling defeated.

For a time I really thought I wanted to die, and then I considered how sad my mother would be if she came home and found me dead and buried. She had often told me I was all she had, the one person she loved. Once, in a rare moment of despair, she had cried: "I would have given up long ago, if it wasn't for you."

Now in the darkness I wondered why my mother's life had turned out so badly. She had been brought up by an aunt who, she said, had never understood her. I remembered what Patsy had told me about my mother's search for the home she had loved before the crash. Perhaps, I thought, she was looking for a haven. In the last three years she had worked in a pub, a café, an office, a pottery place, and a book shop, but none of these jobs had satisfied her and the places we had rented had all been grotty. Each time she started a new job she was full of hope. She would sing merrily, as she cooked in some miserable corner or kitchen. She would buy us both new clothes at the end of the first week and hire a television set. Sometimes she left the job because she didn't like me to be alone in the holidays. Then she would draw social security and we would be together until the next term started, and then she would take another job. She always seemed able to find work, although she had never finished her studies on account of marrying my father. But they weren't very good jobs, nothing, she said, which exercised her mind. She was always bored.

"Oh Katerina," she would say, "wouldn't it be fun to leave, just pack up and go. Would you like that? I'm tired of this place, aren't you? Shall we go north, south, east or west?"

And, of course, I would say: "Yes," for the lodgings were always horrible and I never seemed to settle in any of the schools, and if there was a bottom of the class that would be my place.

Turning all this over in my mind, I forgot my sorrows and drifted into a dreamless sleep, and when I wakened in the morning the sun was shining. All the rain drops glistened like lovely glass beads and a thrush sang in the mulberry tree. I stood looking out of the window and my heart seemed to lift, as my mother's must so often have lifted. with a new hope. And I said aloud to the shining golden world outside:

"I'm going to find the person who sold Cassidy to Arabella. I'm going to get at the naked truth." For a moment I felt very dramatic and rather grand.

Then Patsy called from downstairs that she was going, and I ran into the passage and asked whether the dinner party was all right. She said the grouse had been first rate and that her American friend had never eaten game before and was much impressed.

"He said I was a swell cook," she called, laughing at me from the bottom of the stairs. "Tonight we are going to talk about your reading problem," she said. "Have a good day at the riding school."

A moment later I heard her revving up her mini, and then the crunch of tyres on the gravel as she left.

I went downstairs and looked at my mother's postcard and made myself toast, and hoped that she would phone again. I thought of all the interesting things that I would tell her if she did, and wished that I had been quicker witted the last time.

Then, breakfast finished, I stuffed the postcard in my

48

pocket and went across to see Matthew. He was in the kitchen boiling himself an egg.

"Penelope rang last night, so I told her about the grouse and she said Patsy was very welcome to it."

"Fine, I'm so glad," I said. "But I've got an idea. Who were the people who sold Cassidy to Arabella? You said there was a catalogue."

"I told you, it was a sale, about twelve miles from here. Why don't you ask Arabella? She will have broken up by now." Matthew took his brown egg out of the saucepan and put it in a yellow egg cup.

"I've met her and I have the impression she doesn't exactly like me mucking about with her pony. I used the wrong brush on his tail."

"As if it matters when he has only a few more weeks. Honestly, some people . . . Do you want an egg, by the way?"

I said I didn't, thank you. And Matthew sat down at the kitchen table and shared his breakfast with Tao. Then Mrs. Carter arrived.

"And who might this be?" she asked, looking me up and down as though I was a stray cat who had wandered in from the back of beyond.

"I'm Katerina Turgenieff," I began.

"A Russian *émigrée* whose mother has gone to Russia to look for her husband," chanted Matthew. "She's staying with Mrs. Cooper. And she's not a freak."

"And what's she doing here?"

"I've come to ask Matthew's advice," I replied, looking the fat, square-faced woman straight in the face.

"She wants to save Cassidy, the bay pony," put in Matthew. "She wants to know why he bucks like a bronco."

"Well, it stands to reason, don't it," said Mrs. Carter, leaning on a broom. "He was given the name wasn't he, Hopalong Cassidy. Well, you don't get given a name like that unless you're in the Wild West business, do you?"

"Ah, but was he named Cassidy before or after he was backed? That is the crucial question. He might have been called that because he acted like a bucking bronco. D'ye know the name of the auctioneers who run the horse sales

49

by any chance, Mrs. Carter?" continued Matthew, chucking his egg shell into the sink tidy.

"Well, it's the big ones what do most of the auctions, isn't it? Birmingham people," said Mrs. Carter, still leaning on the broom. " 'ang on, let me think a minute."

We sat very still then, waiting, and Tao put her head on my knee and gazed up at me with her alert brown eyes, and I ran my fingers through the fur on her neck which was like a lion's ruff and lovely to feel.

"Archer, Plugg and Pinkney, that's the firm," announced Mrs. Carter triumphantly, beginning to sweep the floor.

"Right, we'll ring them up." Matthew picked up a telephone directory and threw it to me. "Katie, look them up, will you?" I felt my stomach turn over, then a blush ran right across my face as though a waft of hot air from some furnace had come through the window which was open to the garden. Everyone was finding me out.

"What's the matter? You look as though someone has pulled the rug from under your feet," said Matthew, and then Mrs. Carter stopped sweeping and looked at me, too.

"You're a nail biter," she said. "Terrible, hardly anything left. Someone should have put mustard on them nails when you were small. Don't they 'ave mustard in Russia?"

I handed the telephone directory to Matthew and said: "Please will you look it up?" in a little voice which didn't seem to belong to me at all.

"Can't you read then?" said Mrs. Carter beginning to sweep again. "It's the modern teachers what do it, letting the kiddies do what they want, instead of setting them down at a table and making them work. There's a lot of illiterate people around and this government doesn't want to know."

Matthew found and dialled the number.

"More discipline is what's needed," said Mrs. Carter, picking up the dustpan. "Teachers! All long hair and theory these days!"

"I don't suppose you could manage Russian," I said on a sudden wave of inspiration.

"But I don't need Russian, do I? It's not my country, is

50

it?" Mrs. Carter leaned down to gather the dust and crumbs into the pan.

Matthew was talking. "Yes, of course we can come and see you. No, there's no complaint, nothing like that at all, a very minor matter. Well, that's most kind. Two o'clock then, great. Thank you so much. Yes, Mr. Trumpington is the name. Yes, like the Mayor in Toy Town. Yes, that's right. Yes, thank you. Goodbye then."

"We're to go and see Mr. Plugg," said Matthew, when he had put down the receiver, "two o'clock."

"It's a good thing your voice has broken. You sound quite the gentleman now," said Mrs. Carter.

"He doesn't know exactly what we want," said Matthew. "I just said we were making enquiries about a splendid pony which they sold to Sir Stanley Petworth. And he said that Sir Stanley was one of their most valued customers and he would do what he could to help. He seemed to think I was acting for Sir Stanley, but I never said that at all."

"Grown-ups seem to believe what they want to believe. They jump to conclusions," I said thinking of Patsy and the riding school.

"That's very true," said Mrs. Carter, looking at me approvingly at last.

"What time does the next bus go to Solihull?" asked Matthew.

Mrs. Carter said it went at half-past ten.

"Well, we might as well go then and catch a train into Birmingham and make a day of it," said Matthew.

"And does your mother know about this, this Russian girl?" asked Mrs. Carter.

"Oh yes," said Matthew. "I told her on the telephone. "She was thrilled, you know she loves foreigners."

"I'm English," I said. "I feel English. Please don't call me a foreigner. I belong here."

"Have you got a British passport?" asked Mrs. Carter.

"No. I don't think so. I'm not sure. I may be on my mother's."

"Well then, if you were born in Russia, that's what you are, a Rusky."

"It's much more exotic to be Russian," said Matthew. "They are rare here."

"But I only speak English. I don't remember Russia," I argued. "I was a baby in arms. Ask Patsy."

"Well, come on, let's go. Don't let's argue. Have you got any money?" Matthew reached for his hugger jacket. I said: "Yes," and went to the lodge and fetched the pound Patsy had given in exchange for the elbow grease I had used on the stained glass.

Cassidy was standing under a tree, looking very beautiful with his glistening white star and large dark eyes. I waved to him and he whinnied, and for a moment I thought he was more important than all the books I couldn't read.

Birmingham was hot, dusty and crowded, and Matthew insisted that we went to the new shopping centre, because he wanted to visit the pet shop. We glided grandly down escalators and passed a cage of birds in a passage-way between New Street Station and our destination. Then we spent ages in the shop, while Matthew looked at snakes and tame mice and poor little finches. I talked to the puppies and kittens who gazed at me eagerly from behind wire mesh as though trying to say: "Buy me, buy me." And of course, I longed to buy them all. But even the cheapest, a miserable looking ginger kitten, was a pound and I only had sixty-five pence left after paying train and bus fares.

At last Matthew bought some terrapin and fish food, a pound of sunflower seeds for Rex and a rubber bone for Tao. Then we went back to New Street Station by escalator, and he bought us two pizzas at a restaurant. He said his parents gave him two pounds a week pocket money, so he wasn't exactly poor.

"What about you, Katie?"

I replied that mine fluctuated. Sometimes I might have a pound, other times nothing, and Matthew said it must be very awkward not knowing, as obviously that meant I couldn't plan ahead. This seemed to me rather a strange comment, because planning ahead had never been part of my life, and I reflected then that Matthew was in some ways very old for his years, older in fact than my mother who was thirty-three.

We arrived at the offices of Archer, Plugg and Pinkney at five minutes to two and were told to wait in a small room which looked out on an alleyway. This was in an older part of Birmingham with handsome doorways and porticoes, and an air of lost grandeur about it.

"You had better do most of the talking, because girls are better at coping with people when it comes to a question of appealing for help," said Matthew.

A moment later a small pale secretary with sticking-out teeth and spectacles ushered us into some inner sanctum.

"Mr. Plugg will see you now."

We went into a large office with an important looking table covered in red leather with gold tooling. Behind this sat a round faced man who stared at us, good naturedly, through a pair of glasses, like a kindly toad after a nice meal of worms.

"Well, now," he said, "my appointment book tells me I am to see a Mr. Trumpington."

"That's me," said Matthew with disarming simplicity.

"And what is your connection with Sir Stanley Petworth?"

Although Mr. Plugg was still beaming at us good naturedly, I thought I detected a faint note of irritation in his voice.

"It's about a pony he bought for his daughter at an auction at the end of March," said Matthew, forgetting that he had wanted me to do the talking.

"Under warranty?"

"No, unbroken."

"It's too late to bring any complaint," said Mr. Plugg, fingering a pencil.

"Yes, of course. We just want the name and address of the owner who sold the pony. We want to trace his history."

"He's going to be destroyed, you see," I said quickly. "We want to save his life," and the next moment I had poured the whole miserable story out to Mr. Plugg.

"There's no cause for complaint, you see," I finished, "because he was bought unbroken."

"Although they were not to know that he was unbreakable," put in Matthew with the ghost of a grin.

"Well, I have a daughter who rides," said Mr. Plugg, "and I understand how you feel. You're obviously very fond of the pony."

He pressed a bell and his secretary came back. "Please can you find the catalogue of our March sale. There must be one floating around somewhere."

"Oh yes, in the file, Mr. Plugg," replied the girl, before retreating again.

She came back with a catalogue which Mr. Plugg thumbed through.

"Here we are, Hopalong Cassidy. Bay gelding 13.3 hands, five years old. Unbroken, warranted sound. Owned by Watts and Curling Ltd., of Rugby.

"Where's that?" I asked.

"Next stop after Coventry on the London route," said Matthew promptly. "Thank you Mr. Plugg."

"Good luck with the detective work," said the estate agent, getting to his feet, "and give my regards to Sir Stanley when you see him."

"Yes, of course," we said, "and thank you very much."

"It's strange that he should be owned by a company," remarked Matthew, as we walked back to the station.

He bought a newspaper at the station and split it in half.

"To read on the way back," Matthew said handing me the middle pages. "And keep your eyes skinned for a mention of Watts and Curling Ltd., anywhere in any context."

We sat side by side, and after a bit Matthew said: "You're not reading," and I said, "No, that's right, I prefer looking out of the window."

"Is Mrs. Carter right? Are you illiterate?"

"I don't know what illiterate means," I replied, beginning to bite my nails.

"It means you can't read." He stared me straight in the face, his thick brows raised.

"That's me," I said, turning away to look out of the window again.

"A Russian illiterate," he gave a little grin.

Then suddenly I couldn't take any more. "Oh, go

away," I shouted. "Go away and shut up. You are the most self-satisfied person I've ever met." I threw my bit of the newspaper at him and moved to another seat. I was sweating and my hands were shaking. A moment later I glanced at Matthew and saw that his face was hidden by the newspaper which he had put together again. One or two people in the carriage seemed to be looking at me rather oddly, and I realized I had made an exhibition of myself.

At Solihull we got off the train together, and Matthew said: "I'm sorry. I didn't mean to be horrible. I was just incredulous. I think you manage marvellously for someone who doesn't read. You have such a large vocabulary, and I'm sure it isn't your fault. It's the teachers."

"I don't want to talk about it, please," I said.

"All right," he said.

"We'll go to Rugby tomorrow," he added a moment later, as we waited at the bus stop. "I can pay your fare."

"No, thank you, I'll pay my own. I'm not a pauper," I said.

"I mean I'd lend it to you until your mother comes back. You said you only had sixty-five pence left. I'm trying to be practical, that's all."

"Yes, of course," I said, very tight-lipped and grand, "but I'd rather find the money myself. I can earn it tonight I daresay. I don't need a loan, thank you all the same."

"I'm sorry, I'm sorry I mentioned the reading," said Matthew. "The Russian alphabet is quite different isn't it? You must find things hard."

"You're being false. My mother would find you false," I said remembering Patsy's words. "Because you know I came over as a baby. I told you that. You're being hypocritical. I can't read Russian either. I'm a right fool!"

"I had forgotten, I'm sorry," said Matthew quite humbly. "Why don't you let me teach you to read?"

"Well, if teachers can't teach me I don't see how you can."

"Oh, teachers," said Matthew arrogantly. "Some people are no good at teaching in spite of their qualifications. Besides I expect you have been in large classes of forty or more, but I should give you individual attention."

"Well over thirty," I said. "Thank you, Matthew, I'll think about it."

I wanted to add: "I'm sorry to have been so angry," but the words wouldn't come. Another voice inside me said that I had already been humiliated. Why grovel?

We parted outside Patsy's gate, and I went to talk to Cassidy, who searched my pockets for titbits and ran his muzzle through my hair. I liked him because he was beautiful and because he liked me and, most of all perhaps, because I simply felt at home with ponies. He meant more than most humans to me, because he couldn't criticize. He didn't care whether I could read or not. He just knew from my smell and my behaviour that I was a friend who cared for him. And that was enough. It all seemed so uncomplicated.

CHAPTER SEVEN

"GODMOTHERS ARE HERE TO HELP"

"You poor thing, I had no idea," said Patsy, as we sat either side of an oak table drinking after-supper coffee. "I can't think why your mother didn't tell me."

"It doesn't matter," I said. "I manage."

"But it does matter," cried Patsy. "And as your Godmother, I'm going to do something about it. Your mother is totally irresponsible. Hasn't she had you tested for dyslexia?"

"At least two experts at different schools have interviewed me," I said slowly, dragging my fingers away from my mouth. "One suggested a special school for abnormal children which upset my mother, and the other wanted me to talk with an educational something or another."

"A psychologist?" suggested Patsy.

"Yes, that's it," I said.

"And what did your mother say to that?"

"She said I wasn't mad or abnormal so neither solution was satisfactory. She said I was simply suffering from a reading problem. She said I was exceptionally intelligent and used many words without ever learning to read, so I must be bright, and that all the teachers were barking up the wrong tree."

"And what did the experts say to that?" asked Patsy, peering at me eagerly across the table.

"They didn't say anything because we moved house each time, and I changed schools," I said.

Patsy made disapproving noises with her tongue.

"Your naughty mother. She really has behaved very badly."

I sat on my hands so that I wouldn't bite my nails and explained that my mother had hoped to spend the entire summer holidays this year teaching me herself.

"Eight hours a day," I said. "She studied a book on that disease you mentioned—dys . . ."

"Dyslexia," put in Patsy. "It's not a disease, simply an abnormality."

"Yes, well, she said a concentrated effort must be made over a short space of time. And then a letter came and she changed her mind. She said she must go to Russia instead, and so here I am."

"Is she trying to bring back your father?" asked Patsy.

"I don't know, I've no idea. I've told you that."

"I don't suppose she will succeed. The government of the Soviet Union is very stubborn," said Patsy.

I looked up then beyond my Godmother to where a pretty gilded mirror hung on the white wall, and I could see my face, wide and blue-eyed, framed in dark hair. My cheeks were pink and my mouth rather wide and loose and my neck strong and short like a stone pillar, but I wished it was like a swan's, long and delicate, or like Arabella's, graceful and curved.

"I don't look foreign," I said. "I look British."

"You look as though you could be Welsh, Celtic anyway, with that combination of dark hair and bright blue eyes, but I think the width of your face is Russian or East European, there is a sort of strength there, almost a stubbornness," said Patsy thoughtfully. "And you've needed that, tramping from place to place with Maria."

"I would rather look like Arabella," I said. "Golden, like honey."

"Now listen," said Patsy. "I rang a teacher I know and she advised me to telephone a man who copes with children with reading difficulties, and he gave me the name of someone who has studied dyslexic children."

"But it will be expensive," I objected. "We must wait till my mother gets back."

"Let me finish, and don't interrupt or I shall get angry," retorted Patsy. "I'm your Godmother and Godmothers are here to help. I made some very good sales to that American. I stand to reap a thousand pounds profit, and if I can't spare fifty of that to help my Godchild, my only Godchild, I should be ashamed of myself."

"Fifty pounds!" I said horrified. "We could buy Cassidy for that."

"Oh, damn the pony," snapped Patsy. "We're looking at your future."

"It's early-closing day tomorrow, so I'm taking you to see the man. I've made an appointment."

"But I'm going to Rugby," I cried. "I'm going to see about Cassidy's future."

"Rugby? What about Miss Kirk? Isn't she expecting you?"

"Oh, she doesn't mind. She doesn't want me anyway. What's the use of a helper who can't read the appointments book?"

"Oh, you poor child," said Patsy softening again. "But why Rugby?"

"Because I'm going there with Matthew to find the people who sold Cassidy to Arabella's father, so that we can trace his life history, so that we know why he thinks he should be a bucking bronco. We can leave at nine and catch a train from Birmingham International."

"Well, you'll have to go on Thursday instead, because I've made an appointment for two o'clock and you might not get back in time," said Patsy looking very determined. "I'm afraid this time you must do as you're told. The man is doing me a favour."

"I'll have to go and tell Matthew," I said more calmly. "I hope he won't mind."

"Won't tomorrow do?"

"No, he may want to arrange to do something else. I

58

think I ought to let him know straight away, if you don't mind," I said. Now that my awful secret was out, I felt better, almost cheerful, especially as Patsy seemed to think there was a solution.

"Well, off you go then, but don't be long," she said quite good-naturedly. "I'll wash up."

I knocked on Matthew's door and it sprang open to reveal a slim woman with dark, swinging hair, touched with auburn, a gash of a mouth and expressive hazel eyes, vaguely familiar because I had seen her on television and her eyes resembled Matthew's.

"My dear, you must be the little Russian girl. Come in, how nice." She took an elegant step backwards to allow me room. She was wearing a patchwork skirt and a red blouse open at the throat, and her smile showed a set of perfect teeth. Feeling small and awkward, I scuttled in like an overgrown mouse.

"I just wanted to cancel tomorrow, that's all," I said.

"Oh, hullo, Katie," called Matthew from upstairs. "I recognized your voice. I'll be down in a minute."

"A drink," suggested Mrs. Trumpington in a voice which I can only describe as golden. "Coke, or bitter lemon, squash or ginger beer?"

"Oh, nothing, thanks."

"Sit down, make yourself at home. Matthew has been telling me all about you. What an adventurous life you've led, a nomad always on the move, very romantic, but unsettling I should imagine."

I found myself biting my nails and hastily sat on my hands again.

"Well, yes and no. You know it can be awkward, no fixed address and all that sort of thing. It's not much good for making friends."

"Or keeping belongings. Matthew says you have no belongings."

"No, I suppose I haven't," I agreed, blushing for the thought had not occurred to me before, and made me feel like a tramp.

"But you would like Cassidy to be a belonging?"

"Oh no," I said aghast. "I haven't any money to buy

him with. I just want to save him from being killed and fed to hounds. He's so sweet with all his life before him."

"Let me get you a drink, please let me. I should love to have one myself," said Mrs. Trumpington, looking at me imploringly with her lovely eyes which had just a touch of green in the brown, like autumn leaves before the first frost.

"Oh, all right then," I agreed not very graciously, for I felt hideously embarrassed by the whole conversation. "I should love a coke."

"Which will rot your teeth," said Matthew coming in. "Shall I get them Penelope? What's yours?"

"A gin and bitter lemon, darling," said Mrs. Trumpington, smiling up at her son. "How nice it is to be home. Matthew tells me you have a reading problem and we were wondering how we could help. I know a marvellous man in London. He is an absolute sweetie, and with the patience of an angel."

"Oh, it's all right," I said hastily. "Honestly, Patsy's fixed up something."

"Oh, that's fine," said Mrs. Trumpington. "Oh, I am glad. Heavens, I think you're brave. Coming here all by yourself to live with a woman you haven't seen since you were two, with your mother miles away in Russia. You've certainly got guts!"

"Oh, I don't know," I said after a pause. "Patsy's great and she's got such a friendly cat called Felix. He welcomes me every morning."

"Yes, cats are sweet. I would like a marmalade one like Orlando—you know in the book—but of course we can't because of Rex."

"And then there's Cassidy," I went on. "He's great company. I always feel at home with ponies. Mummy says it's all to do with reincarnation. She really believes I was a pony last time, and she thinks she may have been a lost cat, because she's so restless."

"What a fascinating idea," said Mrs. Trumpington taking her gin and bitter lemon from Matthew. "Your mother sounds such fun. I'm sure we would love her if only we could meet."

"Well, she's a fairly original sort of person. I mean she's

not quite like anyone else. She's full of ideas," I said, "and very witty."

There was indeed something about Mrs. Trumpington which loosened my tongue, and in no time I had told her a great deal about myself, while Matthew brought down Rex and played with him on the floor, and then fetched some of his kindergarten books to see whether I could manage to read them, but I couldn't.

"And yet you speak so wonderfully. You have such a wide vocabulary. Why, your I.Q. must be phenomenal," said Mrs. Trumpington. "Aren't teachers ridiculous, the way they fail to recognize talent?"

"You're probably an extra gifted child," said Matthew.

I thought that was going a bit far and wondered whether they were teasing me, but they looked in deadly earnest, so I cheered up.

"Some very clever people suffer from dyslexia; it's nothing to do with intelligence," Mrs. Trumpington assured me. "What I like about you, is your incredibly open mind. You see every question from several sides, now that is quite rare in someone of thirteen."

"That's only because my mother does," I retorted, not wanting to take the credit. "I'm only copying her, but it has its disadvantages."

When I returned to the lodge, Patsy said: "I did ask you not to stay too long."

"They didn't want me to go. Mrs. Trumpington talked and talked. She was so interested in everything that I couldn't leave before without being rude."

"Well, are you going to Rugby on Thursday instead of tomorrow then?"

"Oh heavens," I cried.

"You forgot all about it," suggested Patsy with a sigh. "You'd better phone Matthew. There's the directory, you can look up his number."

"You know I can't," I said, but not miserably, because somehow Mrs. Trumpington had made me feel rather fine.

"Oh no, bring it here. The sooner we get you reading the better. It's like having a tot in the house," said Patsy, with a nice smile which turned her words into a joke.

Matthew said Thursday would do just as well, and I went to bed feeling that the old saying that a trouble shared is a trouble halved was probably absolutely right.

I dreamed that I was lunging Cassidy when my mother turned up carrying a baby in a shawl. "I went to Russia to make another you," she said, "only this time he's turned out to be a boy, so I've called him Matthew, because I know you can read that word, and what's the good of having a brother if you can't read his name."

I wakened to see the first grey light of dawn and then the sun rising on quilted pink clouds which ripened into red. I lay watching, for my window faced east, feeling snug and comfortable under my flowered duvet in Patsy's little spare room with the carved oak chest and the Jacobean chair. I thought: "Why, your I.Q. must be phenomenal," and "You see every question from several sides and that is quite rare in someone of thirteen." They like me, I decided. They really do. Both Matthew and Penelope. And I had thought they wouldn't want to know me once they realized I was illiterate. Now I wondered what my mother would think of the new friends I had made without any help from anyone.

CHAPTER EIGHT

WE LOSE REX

"How did it go with the expert?" asked Matthew when we were sitting beside each other in the train going to Rugby.

"Oh, all right," I replied, "he's passing me on to someone else, who will take me for two hours a day, five days a week, and I shall have homework on top of that. I suppose it will open a new world to me, rather like a partially-blind person being able to see colours at last, or something. I'm trying to look on the bright side. My first lesson is tonight."

"I'll help you," offered Matthew with a grin. "I trained Tao from a puppy, as well as Rex, and you must admit they're both pretty good, so I don't see why I shouldn't train you."

I pushed him with my foot. "I'm not an animal," I said, laughing.

The train stopped at Coventry, and I told Matthew how I had failed to recognize Birmingham International on the way over.

"It must be jolly hard to find your way around if you can't read signposts or notices," he said. I explained that I had developed a special sense of direction and a capacity for remembering landmarks.

"Once I've been to a place, I can usually find my way there again," I finished.

"Like a horse or dog," said Matthew, laughing again. "But then you were a horse last time, weren't you? My mother loves that theory. She obviously likes you."

"Oh, I had a letter from Russia this morning," I said, wanting to change the subject, "and I'm wondering whether you could read it for me. I expect Mummy thinks Patsy will do that, but she has always left when I get up. She prefers it that way, because she likes to be on her own first thing in the morning. She says she's half asleep and acts like a zombie, and my presence would put her off-centre, so she likes me to get up afterwards."

"It comes from living alone; I expect she's formed habits," said Matthew, while I dug in my pockets.

"Here we are."

A handful of Scott's oats flew out with the letter.

"What on earth . . .?" began Matthew looking nervously at the two dark-suited men sitting opposite us.

"It's all right. I bought a bag of Scott's Porage Oats for Cassidy. I give him a handful when he's good, and keep some in my pocket for emergencies."

I watched one of the men brushing a few flakes from his trouser legs. "I'm sorry. I suppose it was a bit uncivilized. I do apologize," I added to the carriage in general.

"I'm sure Arabella doesn't do things like that," said Matthew, taking the letter. "She's too well brought up."

"Do you know her?"

"Well, sort of. We've met occasionally at local parties. I used to have a great friend at school. He came round every evening. Then his parents moved and he had to go too. He writes but it isn't the same."

"And he knew Arabella?"

"Yes, he was rather smitten, actually. When she had a cousin staying we went to see films a few times as a foursome."

"What was the friend's name?"

"The girl was called Pip, short for Phillipa, and the boy Thomas."

"And you miss Thomas?"

"I do a bit."

"Was the girl pretty?"

"Oh, marvellous," replied Matthew grinning. "Long blonde hair, dazzling eyes and a beauty queen's figure."

"You're joking."

"Well. you asked for it, didn't you?"

"The train's stopping," I cried. "Come on, this must be Rugby."

"All right, don't panic, plenty of time," drawled Matthew, getting up and putting on his hugger jacket, which had a bulge in one of the pockets, "You haven't bought a coat. What will you do if it rains?"

"Get wet. Come on, hurry." I pulled his arm. "You'll have to open the door. I can't manage them."

"In these modern high-speed trains the art is to open the window first," said Matthew coolly. "Then reach down for the handle."

A moment later we were on the platform and the train was gliding away like a blue and grey python.

"My letter? We left the letter!" I cried, aghast.

"Oh heavens! What clots we are! It was my fault, I put it down," said Matthew.

"But it was my letter, I should have remembered it," I said.

"We'll ring up tonight and see if anyone's handed it in," suggested Matthew. "Come on, it's no good crying about it."

But it turned out to be one of those days when nothing works out right and everything goes wrong.

Stupidly we had imagined that it would be quite easy to find the offices of Watts and Curling Ltd. First of all we hopefully asked a few people around the station whether they knew of the firm and they all said no. Then Matthew said we must look in a local telephone directory, so we found a kiosk and, after waiting for ages for a young girl who seemed to be having an interminable conversation, we got inside ourselves. Matthew thumbed through the directory with great expertise.

"Here, Watts and Curling, address and all. Great!" he cried in next to no time. "Now shall we phone first? It might be sensible because then they can tell us the way."

"Yes, do," I said. Then, as Matthew turned back to the phone, I saw a little brown head and a pair of boot-brown eyes.

"Oh you haven't brought Rex!" I cried.

"Why not? He was awake and didn't want to be left. He likes travelling with me. Didn't you notice him in the train sniffing the air when those porridge oats flew about?"

I had to admit that I hadn't.

"He likes travelling in my pocket," added Matthew laughing gaily as he dialled a number.

"Hullo, hullo! Oh bother, it's giving the unobtainable sound. I'll try 'enquiries'."

"Enquiries" said there was no one using that number at the present time, and that Watts and Curling were not listed at any other number.

"We'll copy down their address and call round. Perhaps a shop next door can tell us where they've gone. It's interesting to note that they were Watts and Curling Entertainments Ltd., here," he said writing down the address on a crumpled bit of paper from his pocket. "Right, come on."

I remembered that there had been some kind of map outside the station and, on returning, we found it showed the streets of the centre of Rugby, and in a few minutes we had decided roughly how we would go to the address.

"We are bound to find something," said Matthew cheerfully. "Let's buy some chocolate."

We dived into a newsagents, just as it started to rain, where a fat woman beamed at us from behind a counter bright with confectionery.

We started to choose which bars to have, and the very next moment I saw the woman's flabby face contort into an expression of horror and fear, her brown eyes like sultanas which have swollen in a cake.

"Oh no, go away. Go out at once! I won't have one of those on my premises. Out d'ye hear? Out!"

"He's a tame rat, terribly nice and absolutely hygienic, bred under the cleanest conditions . . ." began Matthew, pushing Rex back.

"Out," screamed the woman, waving her arms like a frightened hen flapping her wings before taking flight. "Away with you, bringing a rat into my nice clean shop! I'll have the police after you."

Outside Matthew said: "Idiot, uncivilized idiot. Honestly a grown-up woman, can you believe it?" And he brought out Rex and stroked his head. "Don't take any notice, humans like that need to have their heads examined. What a way to treat a well-bred Norwegian gentleman."

"I'll go in by myself next time. You stay outside," I suggested.

"Here's a fifty-pence piece," said Matthew.

"No thanks, I've plenty of money. I cleaned up lots of absolutely filthy objects last night for Patsy, and she pays me for my work," I said.

Presently we were on our way again munching fruit-and-nut chocolate, which we shared with Rex.

"Everything's going to be all right. I have a feeling in my bones," said Matthew pushing back his hair. "We're going to save Cassidy and your mother is going to come back with your father, and they're going to buy a house and you're all going to live happily ever after."

"And they're going to buy Cassidy, I suppose. Oh Matthew, that would be too good to be true!" I said. "Things like that just don't happen."

"Yes, I suppose so. I say, aren't you getting rather wet?"

"Not really, it's warm rain," I said.

"Would you like my jacket? It's not exactly waterproof, but it's better than nothing."

"No, I think Rex had best stay with you. He might take a flying leap or something awful if I took over the jacket."

Soon the rain was splashing round our feet and I could

feel my striped shirt clinging to my body, and our hair hung in soaking strands, and rain dripped off our noses.

"Can you remember where we turned at the bridge?" asked Matthew. "Somehow that screaming woman made me forget the last part of the route."

"I think left, but I'm not sure. What was the name of the street. Can you remember? St. something."

"Hang on," said Matthew. "Move Rex. Oh heavens!" He stopped, holding in his hand a few tattered bits of paper. "Rex has been eating the address. Look." He held up the remains. "I didn't memorize it because I had written it down and I wanted to concentrate on remembering the route. Can you?"

"I thought you were, I'm dreadfully sorry."

We stood and looked at one another and very bedraggled we were by then. Matthew tried to put the pieces of paper together, but too much had been eaten. "We had better go into that café over there, and have a cup of coffee and think what to do next. We must be nearly there," he said, still smiling.

It was a dark, cheerless place with chipped orange walls and brown formica tables and worn lino on a concrete floor. But the fat moustached man behind the counter smiled at us in so welcoming a manner that Matthew said: "I hope you don't mind, but I have a pet rat in my pocket."

"Oh, we must see him," the man said at once. "Lovely little pets rats make. 'Old on, I'll get 'im a nibble of cheese. Sit down by the fire and dry yourselves while I shut our puss in. You're soaked to the skin." We pulled two chairs up by a one-bar electric fire, and Matthew brought out Rex and stroked him. The rat stood up on his hind legs, in a begging position, and sniffed the air, his whiskers trembling. "He likes travelling," Matthew said.

" 'Ere we are, 'ow's this for the little fellow?" The man came back and handed us a piece of cheddar cheese. "I must tell the wife. She loves animals; proper conservationists we are," he added.

We spent fifteen minutes in that café drinking rather nasty coffee and eating biscuits. The café owner lent us his directory and we looked up the address again and he

67

explained the way to us. Soon we set off again in better spirits.

We found the street but the office was shuttered-up and the metal plate which had once boasted the name of Watts and Curling Entertainments Ltd., was tarnished and barely readable. We banged on the door and rang the bell in vain.

"We've drawn a blank," Matthew said. "Now what shall we do?"

"Go home," I said.

"Never say die," replied Matthew.

"I'm wet and cold," I said.

"Into those offices. Come on," cried Matthew. "We can at least try."

We went up in an old-fashioned lift that clanked, and knocked at a door.

"Come in."

We pushed open the door and went in.

A trim young woman, in a white clinging sweater and yellow flowered skirt, said: "Can I help you?"

"Watts and Curling Entertainments," said Matthew. "The place next door."

"I beg your pardon." Her eyes grew larger, like a frightened deer's.

"Do you know where they've gone, please?"

"Haven't a clue. Sorry."

"Did they go bust?"

"Probably."

"What did they do?"

"I say! Are you carrying out an investigation or something?"

"Yes," I replied. "We are trying to save a pony from death, a pony they owned, a beautiful pony called Cassidy. Please help us." I sounded dramatic and Matthew made a deprecating gesture, which seemed to say don't get excited.

"I'll ask Maisie, she's been working here donkey's years. She might know; she likes ponies," the girl said getting up to teeter away on incredibly high heels.

"Quiet Rex. Get down you little monkey!" said Matthew, pushing back the small brown face peeping from under his pocket flap.

68

"You must expect him to want to know what's happening," I said.

The girl returned with a red-haired woman of middle age, with freckles and very large, blue-grey eyes.

"Entertainment people, that's what they were," Maisie said. "Provided shows at fêtes and carnivals."

"Wild West shows, that sort of thing?" I asked rather breathlessly.

"Yes, they used to put on a rodeo show, with prizes for those who stayed on the longest."

"On the broncos, you mean?" asked Matthew.

"Yes, that's it, that's it in a nutshell. I saw them once at a carnival in Birmingham. Lovely little ponies they were, but buck! I've never seen anything like that before or since! It surprised me no one was hurt. The way they threw their riders up in the air! The Wild West films on telly are nothing compared with that, not when it comes to bucking. And I know something about it because I've got a horse-mad daughter."

"Oh, bad luck!" exclaimed Matthew with a laugh. "That's all we need to know, thank you very much, and it bears out your hunch, Katie. Little Cassidy thinks he is doing the right thing when he chucks people off."

"Oh, they were well trained," Maisie said. "Set to bucking the moment the corral gate was opened, and then stopped and stood as good as gold once the rider was off."

"You don't know whether the firm has an address anywhere else," asked Matthew.

"No way," Maisie said. "They were there one day and gone the next. A moonlight flit, if you ask me."

"We know his history now," I said. "Thank you both very much."

"What's that?" Maisie asked. "That little face looking out of your pocket? You haven't brought a rat in here, have you?"

"It's Rex, a hooded Norwegian rat, hygienically bred, clean as the cleanest kitten and twice as intelligent. Here, Rex."

"You can count me out," said the girl in the tight white sweater, getting behind a table.

"He's rather sweet," Maisie said. "Look at those

whiskers." She stroked Rex and he looked up at her enquiringly and then made the little crooning noise that he used when he was pleased and loving.

"Matthew we must go. I've got a reading lesson tonight," I said. "Please."

"A reading lesson at your age!" exclaimed Maisie.

"She's Russian. They have a different alphabet," Matthew said. "Back you go, Rexy dear."

"Half Russian," I said.

Out in the street, Matthew said: "Mission completed. Day turned out all right after all. Hi, stop! Rex!"

But he was too late, for in the same instant the rat took a leap from his pocket, landed on a wall and disappeared through railings down into a basement area.

"Oh, my God!" cried Matthew in great anguish.

We climbed over the locked basement gate just in time to see the little rat disappear into a drain which seemed to lead nowhere.

"Rex, Rex, Ratty, Rexy. Come on, here, come on, cheese!" called Matthew. "Chocolate—seeds!"

But the rat didn't come. Soon we went back up the steps and climbed the next gate into the next basement area, but without avail. The rat had disappered. This was a run-down part of the town and, apart from the office block, most of the buildings were empty. awaiting demolition.

"He could be anywhere," said Matthew, in a small tight voice, and at that very moment a large black and white cat went by on soft, noiseless pads. "There are so many gaps and holes that he could be in one of the houses. He moves so fast when he's excited. Oh, go away, you horrible cat. Go on. Go!"

It began to rain, softly, the drops falling soundlessly like the tears of an old woman who has no strength left for sobbing.

"Ratty, Rex!" called Matthew again.

"He's being a real rat," I said.

"What do you mean?" exploded Matthew.

"Well, running down drains and things, exploring. He might find a Mrs. Rat, perhaps he has smelt one," I suggested.

"Oh no," wailed Matthew. "Don't say that. He hasn't

been bred to live outdoors. He feels the cold. He needs cherishing. He's bred for the constant temperature of a laboratory. Don't you understand?"

"Yes, and I'm so sorry," I said putting a hand on Matthew's arm.

"You had better go back," he said. "You've got your lesson, and Patsy will be fussing."

"Can't I help?"

"No, please go. You're getting soaked. Why didn't you bring a coat? Honestly, sometimes I think girls have been born without sense."

"No, it's just me, not all girls," I said, feeling stupidly humble. "I'll go then, if that's what you want."

"Yes, it is," said Matthew, and I guessed then that he needed to face this problem alone, that anything I could say would only irritate him, and that if we found Rex dead I should cry and make things worse.

Feeling hopeless and bedraggled, I walked away up the street.

CHAPTER NINE

CASSIDY DISAPPEARS

My teacher was young, moustached, dark-haired and encouraging, but I read badly because I was worrying about the rat and Matthew. As soon as I was home again, I ran round to the Trumpingtons' cottage to see whether Matthew was back. He wasn't. Then I went to see Cassidy, wondering what I could do now that I knew he had been trained to buck. How could I make him realize that he must change his career and become a riding pony?

A handful of Scott's oats in my pocket, I called: "Cassidy, Cassidy. Come on, up. Come on."

The rain pattered on my bare head and the trees dripped, and there was no answering whinny.

"Oh Cassidy, where are you?"

My voice was full of weary entreaty. The day had already been too long, too full of anxiety and disappointment. The triumph of finding out the pony's past had been muted by the loss of Rex, and Matthew's despair.

"Cassidy, where are you? Come on. Come up!"

The silence was awful; no swish of equine legs coming through the grass, no squelch of hoofs by the gate where the mud showed darkly through the greenness of the pasture. The place was empty; the field deserted apart from a few sparrows chirruping noisily in the white hawthorn. Cassidy had gone! The knackers, I thought.

Oh no! The knackers! We're too late! They have killed him. In my mind's eye, I saw a long trough; hounds eating greedily, fighting over his cannon bones; the kennel huntsman wiping a bloody knife on his white coat.

I ran back to the cottage and hammered on the door, but Matthew had not yet returned. I looked through the letter box. Tao barked. This, I thought, was to be our day of tragedy. The rat gone, the pony gone! My stomach felt light and empty, and there was a familiar pricking behind my eyes. Arabella, I thought suddenly. I would go and find Arabella! I started to run again. I ran wildly across the field, and then the park to the great Georgian house which smiled across the landscape in lovely symmetry. There were pillars by the front door and steps beyond the noble sweep of the gravelled drive. I felt very small and untidy standing and banging the brass knocker, while the peacocks shrieked on the lawn. The rain dripped from my hair, but under my mackintosh I was sweating. Dogs barked, and at last a woman in an overall came.

"Arabella, please may I see Arabella?"

"Abroad," the woman said, "the family are abroad."

"When will they be back?"

"Next week."

"I came about the pony," I explained. "Cassidy."

"The one that broke Miss Arabella's arm, the vicious one," the woman asked.

"That's right."

"Sir Stanley said he was to go to hounds."

"Has he gone?"

"I don't know. I couldn't say. You must ask Mr. Smithers."

"And who is Mr. Smithers, please?" I asked.

"The groom. He's sure to know."

"Is he at the stables?" I began to back away down the steps, wanting to run at once to find the man, not to waste a moment.

"He'll be back at nine," the woman said.

"Nine tonight?"

"Yes, that's it. You can come back then. His cottage adjoins the stables."

"Has he taken the pony to be killed?" I asked. "Have you seen the truck?"

"I don't know. I don't know anything about the horses. I'm not interested, see. But I do know that Cassidy nearly killed the horse breaker and is no good to anyone, no good at all."

"I'll come back," I said, "at nine. Will you tell Mr. Smithers, please? Will you tell him I have some important information about Cassidy, and he simply mustn't be sent to hounds?"

"I'll tell him that," the woman said. "And now you had better go home and dry your hair or you'll catch your death of cold."

I ran back and rubbed my hair with a towel, and wondered whether Matthew had found his rat. Then, remembering that I had missed lunch, I made myself a cup of coffee and talked to Felix until Patsy came back, all smiles because she had made 100 per cent profit on an oak chest, which she had bought at a sale in Hampton-in-Arden.

"Had a good day? How was your reading lesson?"

"Terrible," I said, and told her my tale of woe.

"You can't stop them. He's not your pony," said Patsy.

"I shall try. They must see now that he's not vicious," I argued.

"He's spoiled for life, and a spoiled pony is no good to anyone. You must be realistic," said Patsy. "Whether or not he's to blame doesn't come into it."

"But justice," I began in my mother's voice, "justice demands that he should not be killed by humans simply because he was wrongly trained by humans. You must see that!"

"Animals have no rights. They are exploitable. Cassidy

73

is no longer an employable person, so to speak. He's incapable of earning his keep. You cannot expect Sir Stanley to feed a useless animal through the winter. Now what about supper?"

"I don't want any supper thank you," I said most vehemently. "I'm going to see if Matthew has found Rex. Oh, and by the way, there was a letter from my mother."

"Oh, where? Does she give an address? It's so irresponsible of her not to leave even a telephone number. Supposing you were desperately ill—what should I do? But then your mother never was practical."

"She trusts in fate," I said. "Divine providence or something."

"She needs to. Now let's see the letter. I expect you want me to read it."

I looked at Patsy and then at my feet.

"You haven't lost it, have you? Oh Katie!" cried my Godmother. "When are you going to grow up a bit?"

I turned away, because I didn't want her to see how sad I was. I felt wrung out, bedraggled, like an old-fashioned mop at the end of its days. The rat, the pony and the letter, all lost!

"It might have something important in it, something about the date of her return. I mean I love having you, but you can't stay here for ever. I want to go to Madeira in October, and what is to happen to you then? Tell me that, Katie. The trouble about your mother is . . ." her voice droned on, and outside the rain fell and a blackbird sang in the mulberry bush.

"I'm dreadfully sorry," I said at last. "I left it in the train to Rugby. I'm so worried about Rex. He seems so little and white and vulnerable to be out on his own in a town, and Matthew is so terribly upset."

"But I've got to plan," continued Patsy. "And how can I plan when you lose your mother's letters, so that I don't know what your future is. And what about your schooling? I mean the holidays will soon be over and what then . . .?"

"Oh, it's all too much," I said.

"And now you are over-reacting. You're being melodramatic. I'll ring British Rail Lost Property," said Patsy a little more calmly, as though my reaction had proved to her at last that her words had not been wasted and that I was taking seriously the way in which I was inconveniencing her. "You must tell me about the reading later," she added, going for the telephone directory.

I went back to the cottage and found Matthew sitting with his head in his hands.

"No luck?" I asked.

"Not a sign. I feel so awful. I mean, I shouldn't have taken him. And he thinks all animals are his friends. He will run up to that cat as he runs up to Tao, and then . . ."

"Don't think about it, switch your mind off. I have a blow too. Cassidy has gone!"

"Gone?" Matthew brought his head out of his hands. "Gone where?"

I told him about my enquiries.

"I'll come with you at nine if you like." he said.

"I keep thinking of that little bay head with the shining white star, severed from his body. It's like a nightmare or rather a daymare."

"Penelope comes back tonight; she'll help," said Matthew.

"Everything seems to have hit us at once, and the trouble is that people are so thick. Mention a rat and they laugh or scream depending on their sex. They can't understand that Rex has feelings and fears, and a remarkable intelligence. They are conditioned to think of rodents as vermin, dirty vermin, and it's so unfair, for no one could clean himself more than Rex does, and as for hurting anyone . . ."

"I think my mother is right and there's something very wrong with the human race," I said. "God should never have given them dominion over the animals."

"Oh Katie, I'm too tired to talk philosophy or religion," said Matthew. "I'm going to scramble an egg. What about you?"

"I'll go back," I said. "I told Patsy that I didn't want anything, but perhaps she'll let me change my mind. I feel better now."

At a quarter to nine Matthew and I walked across the park in the early dusk. The rain had stopped but the grass

75

was wet underfoot. The great trees nodded in a gentle breeze shaking down beads of water like diamonds, and overhead the sky was lively with chasing clouds and windows of sudden light.

"I love the sky," I said, "and the moon and all the stars. It's a world of its own."

"You're an extraordinary girl!" exclaimed Matthew. "You are not like anyone else I know."

"I'm glad," I said.

Mr. Smithers was in his red-brick cottage, which did indeed adjoin the stables. A red-cheeked man with bulbous nose and bright blue eyes, he came to his door and stood four-square, looking us up and down.

"Yes, Mrs. Riley did tell me you had called," he said. "And the pony's gone."

"Gone where?"

"You know, you know very well. Miss Arabella wrote you a letter about it."

"I never received it," I said.

"Would have come by this morning's post I reckon," the man replied.

"Are you sure?" asked Matthew, looking at me.

"Well, I don't really look at the letters unless they have a Russian stamp. I put them in a pile for Patsy to see on her return," I admitted. "I might have missed it."

"I suggest you go back and read the letter then," the groom said.

"Couldn't you tell us where?" asked Matthew. "Please. We've come all this way to find out."

"Mrs. Riley said, didn't she? Gone to the hunt to feed hounds. He was no good to anyone, see. A pretty pony I admit, but useless."

"He was taught to buck. He was sold as unbroken, but in fact he had been used as a bucking bronco. Arabella should have realized that when she saw who the sellers were in the catalogue," I said.

"It don't make no difference now. It's all in the past," Mr. Smithers said. "That pony's done a lot of damage, breaking arms and legs and causing concussion. And when Sir Stanley heard you had taken such a liking to him, he said do it now because, sooner or later you'd be

76

climbing on its back and then you might be killed, and he wouldn't want to feel responsible for a little girl's death."

"Oh," I said, feeling like a wrung-out mop again. "Surely not."

"Surely yes," the groom said. "He was to leave it till the winter or at least the autumn, but he was that worried about you. And then we thought it would be best while Miss Arabella was abroad, as she didn't want to see him go."

"So is he dead?" asked Matthew.

"And eaten or cooking," the man said, "He went first thing this morning. Now you go home and read that letter, and let me get back to my television programme, if you don't mind. You can't do anything. It wasn't your pony and, anyway, it's too late. The pony's dead."

I started to cry as we walked back across the park.

"Haven't you anyone, anyone to look after you, to comfort you?" asked Matthew. "Where are your grandparents, your aunts?"

"My grandparents have been dead a long time. I knew they were dead, but not how they had died. Then Patsy told me that they were killed in a car crash when my mother was small. She never speaks of them, and she was their only child. There were no brothers and sisters, and therefore no aunts." I spoke very quietly, so quietly through my tears that I could hardly recognize the voice as mine. It seemed outside myself. Matthew took my hand.

"I feel like crying too," he said, "but males are not supposed to, are they?"

Just at that moment a black cat passed us with a squeaking mouse in its jaws, and my mind turned at once to Rex, running hither and thither in those derelict houses, and I thought of the other cat, the black and white one, walking so noiselessly in Rugby; and for an awful morbid moment imagined Rex clasped like the mouse, alive and terrified in that other cat's jaws.

Matthew pushed a fist across his eyes. "We must find that letter from Arabella," he said in a stifled voice. "There might have been a mistake. We may not be too late. Miracles do happen."

"I saw the Russian stamp and forgot about the others. I

77

mean I didn't expect anyone to write to me; so I just bundled the others together and put them on the table for Patsy."

"You must get your hair permed," said Matthew suddenly. "All the girls are having theirs done. Then it wouldn't look so lank."

"Yes," I said, dismayed. "Yes, I suppose I must. When my mother comes back."

"When's that?"

"I don't know," I said.

"But she must have got a visa for a certain time. I know about these things because Meredith travels such a lot."

"I think it was for a fortnight."

"But she's been much longer."

"Yes, I know. I may be wrong."

"But if she's married to a Russian national things may be different. I do wish I hadn't left that letter on the train. What a disastrous journey that was. I am so sorry."

"It's all right," I said.

"It isn't really," said Matthew, squeezing my hand.

We found Arabella's letter on the hall chest, and Matthew read it aloud.

"Dear Russian," it began. "By the time you get this I am afraid Cassidy will be dead and I will be in Corfu. I am very sorry that it had to be this way but, believe me, that pony is dangerous, and my father is now afraid that you might ride him and get killed. He really can buck! We would not like to feel in any way responsible for an accident. Please do not be too upset. He won't feel anything, and it will all be over in seconds.
                    Yours sincerely,
                    Arabella."

"It doesn't really make any difference," said Matthew, gloomily. "I'm very sorry because I know you sort of loved Cassidy. He was your best friend here. Perhaps one day you'll have one of your own." I stared back at Matthew then, not knowing what to say, thinking only of a corpse and hounds and the field empty, and no one to groom or care for. The days seemed now to stretch interminably ahead.

"I must go back," Matthew said. "I saw the light which means my mother is home, and she'll wonder where I am."

"There's still hope for Rex," I said fighting back tears. "Someone may find him and look after him. Did you leave your number?"

"Oh yes, with the police, the café and the office where we met Maisie. They all promised to do their best. All is not yet lost on that score." Matthew was cheering up a bit. "See you tomorrow then, first thing. And please cheer up."

After he had gone I went upstairs; I threw myself on my bed and with a loud howl of despair burst into tears. I cried for Cassidy and for Rex and, most of all probably, for myself. I cried because my mother had gone away and I didn't know when she was coming back, and I cried also because I was in Patsy's way, a nuisance preventing her from planning her holiday to Madeira. After a time I had no tears left, and then the door opened an inch and Felix slid in. He climbed up on the pillow and rubbed himself against my tear-blotched face and purred, and then I thought about Matthew and what he had said about my hair. Presently I got up, and looking in the mirror, twisted my long straight locks this way and that. I piled them on top of my head and wound them at the back like a bun, and I tried in vain to frizz them out in a sort of Afro hair style. Nothing made me look elegant or beautiful, so I went to the bathroom and borrowed some of Patsy's shampoo and washed my hair. I had just finished when I heard the sound of her mini, as she returned from after-dinner drinks with friends. Then I ran to my bedroom and went down on my knees and asked God to bring back my mother soon and to save Rex, and, if it was not too late, to save Cassidy, too. And after that, I went to bed in a calmer frame of mind.

CHAPTER TEN

A RACE AGAINST TIME

"We mustn't give up," said Penelope stretching out her slim, shapely legs and smiling that radiant smile that had entranced millions of television viewers.

"But we've been assured that the pony's dead," argued Matthew.

"But did the Smithers man actually see him shot?" asked Penelope, turning her brown-green-eyed gaze on her son with the intensity of a searchlight looking for the enemy. "We must not give up until we are sure. The man's word may not be reliable."

"But Arabella's letter," I began.

"She didn't see him shot either," retorted Penelope, reaching for a cigarette which a moment later she returned to the packet unsmoked. "I'll dress and then we'll go to the hunt kennels and check up."

"My mother is a formidable woman, a campaigner," said Matthew, as Penelope swept out of the room in a flowered dressing-gown, bought specially for use in the cottage.

"She's great," I said, "and so kind."

"Yes, when she's here," said Matthew, rather wistfully I thought.

He started to clear away the breakfast things, and then the telephone rang, and he was out of the room in a flash. Putting egg cups in the sink, I heard his voice: "Yes, yes. Oh, I am so grateful. Oh, that's marvellous, absolutely great. Is he all right? In a box? You won't let him escape again, will you? I don't think I could bear that. We'll be round in about half an hour. Thanks very much."

"They've found Rex," he cried, coming back with a great smile splitting his face. "He was in the office, Maisie's office, when she arrived this morning. Must have gone back there to look for us. How's that for intelligence?"

"I'm so glad," I said seizing both Matthew's hands and swinging them up and down. "It's wonderful."

"They don't know how he got there. They wonder if he went up the ventilator shaft. I'll go and tell Penelope. Now dash back to Patsy's and get a mac or anorak or something and then we'll be on our way."

As I went past the field I felt a moment's anguish. The palings seemed ugly without the little bay head looking over them, the bright eyes encouraging me to come across and feed and groom the lonely pony. But perhaps, I told myself, this is going to be a better day, perhaps fate will be on our side.

Ten minutes later we were driving at seventy miles an hour in Penelope's silver Ford Capri on the motorway that led us part of the way to Rugby.

"You see you despaired too soon. The little fellow is wiser than you thought," said Matthew's mother. "You young people are so up and down, so ready to accept disaster or success. You forget that there's a sort of grey area in between."

"Oh please, Penelope, don't give us one of your little homilies," begged Matthew. "Katie is going to have her hair permed. How do you think it should be done?"

"Oh, I don't know, I shall have to look at her properly, something simple but charming, I should think, bringing out that peculiarly Russian flavour to her face."

"Can a face have flavour?" asked Matthew.

"Oh, you know what I mean," said his mother. "What do you think, Katie?"

"I don't know. I can't have it done for a while anyway," I replied, wondering how I could raise the money to pay.

"You don't have to have it done just to please the Trumpingtons," said Matthew with a grin. "It was just an idea, that's all."

We couldn't park near the office block, so Penelope dropped off Matthew and then we cruised round until we saw him come out with a cardboard box in his hand.

"All safe and sound and very pleased to see me after his adventure," said Matthew getting in.

"Shut all the windows before you let him out," said Penelope, "and don't let him get under my feet or there might be an accident. Now for the hunt kennels. Katie, get out that map and look for Little Dorrington, it's about nine miles west of Coventry."

"Pen, dear, Katie can't read," said Matthew.

"Oh yes, how tiresome. I forgot. Well, put that rat back in the box and look yourself."

"I'll nurse Rex," I offered, feeling horribly red in the face.

"What are you going to do with Cassidy, if you do save him?" asked Penelope a moment later, as she donned a pair of outsize, dark glasses.

"Retrain him," I replied promptly.

"How?"

"I don't know yet, but there must be a way. He's been taught to buck, now we must teach him not to buck."

"It sounds simple, but I bet it isn't," said Penelope. "Which way now, Matthew?"

"Hang on a moment. Stop! I'm not sure."

"I can't stop, there's a car on my tail."

"Draw in then."

We came to a halt by a farm gate, and little Rex climbed up my arm and sat on my shoulder peering into my face. After a moment or two he licked my cheek with his warm pink tongue. Then he started to clean himself, licking his paws and then wiping himself with them. Every now and then his whiskers twitched and sometimes he paused to look out of the window, his beady eyes taking in the scenery with great interest.

"I never thought I would become fond of a rat," I said.

"I don't see why not. He's as clever and devoted as any dog," said Matthew. "First left, second right and then left again, after a church, and then there's another eight miles or so of country lanes."

"Right," said Penelope, swinging out into the road again.

Because my mind was on Cassidy and his probable death, the drive seemed endless, and all the time my stomach seemed to be turning over in the most curious way. "It would be so awful if we were two minutes too late. If we heard the gun go off as we turned up the drive," I said. "We should never get over that."

"I can't go any faster," groaned Penelope.

"Humane killers don't make any sound, I believe," added Matthew. "Right here, and then left round by that pub, no left, the smaller road."

"Isn't there an easier way?"

"Yes, but it's five miles longer."

"Well, it might be quicker," suggested Penelope, "These little country roads do slow one up. They're so curly."

"Too late to change now," said Matthew.

A few moments later we caught up with a tractor pulling a trailer, which we followed at crawling pace for a mile, becoming every minute more exasperated. My tummy now seemed to be eating itself with anxiety.

"You're making too much acid. It's nerves," Penelope told me.

"I keep thinking they may be about to do it now," I explained.

"You've said that before. You're repeating yourself like a senile old lady," objected Matthew.

"His little bay head with the white star, think of that cut off," I said. "Think of the gun held to his forehead." I blinked hard.

"Now you are just trying to pile on the agony," said Penelope. "Torturing yourself. Do be calm and sensible. Morbid fantasies won't help and only serve to lower the morale."

At last the tractor turned into a field, and then we sped on at great speed until we were behind a huge truck laden with grit which kept us down to twenty miles an hour.

"What's the time?" I asked.

"Haven't you a watch?"

"Katie doesn't have anything except herself and a few clothes. It's just five past eleven," replied Matthew. "It's best that she should not bury her fears."

"Well, if she can't read, perhaps she can't tell the time," said Penelope, and then I blushed again, wishing they wouldn't talk of me in this way.

"Actually I can more or less," I said.

"Are figures easier than letters?"

"A bit," I said, willing Penelope to concentrate entirely

on her driving to overtake the truck, and forget me and my shortcomings.

At last we came to the kennels and Penelope brought the car to a halt with a crunch in the gravelled driveway.

"I think I shall stay in," I said.

"But why?" asked Matthew.

"She's afraid she might see part of the pony and have nightmares. Yes, we understand," said Penelope with her radiant smile. "We'll ask the preliminary questions."

They went from the drive into the yard, while I stroked Rex and listened to the baying hounds. Presently I saw them talking to a hatchet-faced man in a white coat, then Penelope beckoned for me to join them. I put the rat in the box, most carefully securing the lid, then, after checking that all the car windows were shut, I did as I was bid.

"This is Mr. Dawson, the kennel huntsman," said Penelope. "He says he hasn't had any horses or ponies in for the past fortnight."

"Have we come to the right hunt?" I asked.

"Sir Stanley hunts with us. He's a subscriber, a good supporter, you might say, walked a couple of pups for us last summer. I can't see him sending the pony anywhere else. He's one of the old school. You wouldn't find him trying to realize an asset by selling horseflesh to the knackers, he's not that sort."

"He's in Corfu, so we can't ask him," said Matthew thoughtfuly.

"It could be that his groom is making a spot of money on the side," suggested the kennel huntsman. "Such things have been known. I don't know the man. He's fairly new, I think, came in the spring from Leconsfield Stud."

"So what should we do now?" asked Penelope, switching on that searchlight gaze that Matthew claimed men found irresistible.

"You could try the slaughter-house."

"Which one?"

"Well, Madam, the nearest doesn't take ponies, not officially, anyway. The most likely one is about forty-five miles from here in Upper Beckenham, not far from Northampton. I should try there if I were you."

"Should we phone them?" asked Matthew.

"Might not be wise," said the kennel huntsman after a pause. "If it's been a shady deal for cash, a call might prompt them to kill the animal right away and destroy the evidence."

"We should just turn up then?" suggested Penelope.

"Yes, the chances are the pony will be carcass by now, but you never know your luck," said the kennel huntsman. "Was he fat?"

"Yes," I said. "A little round barrel."

"Pity, no hope then that they might keep him for a week or two to put on a bit more flesh."

"I think we should hurry," I said, beginning to edge my way back to the car, and then stopping to wait politely while Penelope rounded off the conversation and seemed to offer endless thanks.

"We shall have to put in some more petrol," she said, when at last she was starting the car. "And buy some provisions. Heavens, it's twelve o'clock already!"

"Surely we don't need to eat," I cried. "Cassidy's life is at stake."

"Ah, but we must keep up our strength. Otherwise I might crash the car and then where should we be? I know a charming little pub near Northampton. It only means a little detour. We can have a meal there in a matter of minutes. They have a help-yourself arrangement. Delicious salads, stuffed peppers, and yoghurt for pudding. Now, Matthew, right or left?"

"Wait a minute. I haven't quite got my bearings yet."

I turned away then, because I was very angry that I couldn't read, that I was simply someone tagging on and being no use whatsoever. And because I was frightened that Cassidy would die while we ate salads, peppers and yoghurt.

CHAPTER ELEVEN

THE SLAUGHTER-HOUSE

"I feel in my bones that he will be dead," I said, as we saw the abattoir buildings standing on the edge of a large and densely populated village.

"Bones are not reliable." Penelope replied. "Put that rat in the box, Matthew. There are sure to be cats around."

I felt very tense as we drove into the concreted outer yard. It was a very clean place with not a wisp of straw or hay to be seen. A brown cattle truck and a silver metal truck stood side by side. One for the live animals, the other for the carcasses, I decided.

We went through a door to "Reception", and rang a bell on the table in front of us and, after a few moments, a pleasant-faced man in a white coat and grey cap appeared.

"Hullo, can I help?"

Penelope turned to me and raised her brows.

"We're looking for a bay pony called Cassidy. We want to buy him back," I said, and in the same instant wondered where the money was coming from.

"We've had a bay pony in, but I don't know his name, fetched him yesterday from somewhere near Solihull, a nice looking animal, but vicious, caused some bad accidents."

I wanted to say: "Is he still alive?" but the sentence seemed to die in my throat.

"He isn't really vicious, just sadly mistrained," said Matthew, who is rarely lost for a word. I began to bite my nails.

"The groom had no right to sell him; he was supposed to go to the Hunt to feed hounds," Penelope added.

"Oh," said the man, pushing back his cap. "Have I been dealing in stolen property then?"

"You could put it that way," Matthew said.

"The pony didn't belong to Mr. Smithers then?"

"No. He belonged to Sir Stanley Petworth," said

Penelope. "Any money that changed hands should have gone to him."

"Is he dead?" I cried, at last.

"Who, Mr. Smithers?"

"No, the pony, Cassidy."

"Come and look," suggested the cattle slaughterer. "Come and see for yourself."

We went through another door into an inner yard which had four loose boxes and three pens full of cattle. Enormous doors led into the actual slaughter-house.

"We don't want to see him if he's dead. We are not interested in corpses," said Penelope, afraid that the man might have a macabre turn of mind.

"No, no, of course not. We are not monsters here, dear me, no. You're in luck, actually. By rights he should have been killed yesterday, but the chap who does the ponies is down with some bug. I don't touch them myself. There are special rules for horses, you know. They're not like the cattle. They are not allowed to see one of their kind killed or see a carcass. It's all laid down. They are special cases."

"You mean, he's alive?" My voice was barely above a whisper.

"Look over there!"

"Cassidy," I shouted and, at that moment, his head looked over a loosebox door and he whinnied.

In a moment I was patting him, running my hand through his mane and stroking his shining neck.

"We look after them well here," the slaughterer assured us.

"Who was it who said that man was the only animal who remained friends with his victims until the moment he killed them?" asked Penelope. "Was it Samuel Butler?"

But nobody knew; perhaps nobody cared.

"So you want him back," the slaughterer asked at last.

"We don't want him killed," I said.

"And I don't want to be summoned for handling stolen property," the slaughterer assured me.

"No, that's true," agreed Penelope, "that could mean a court appearance, and a lot of unwelcome publicity. Nobody wants that."

"The groom seemed genuine enough. Mind you, I don't

like handling horseflesh much myself, but it's all in the way of trade. You can't turn down good business, not these days. And I reckon we're the most humane place." The slaughterer pushed back his cap again. His face was pleasant and open. "My man," he went on, "has it down to a fine art, talks to the animals all the time, has an arm round their necks and they don't feel anything. They never know what's happening to them. I understand how your kiddy feels."

Cassidy nuzzled my pockets, then took a corner of my shirt in his mouth and playfully sucked it, as a young pony sometimes takes the loose skin of an equine friend. He ran his lips through my hair while the others moved away and talked.

"She's not my daughter actually. She's all alone staying with a Godmother. Her mother is in Russia and she's never met her father. This pony has been her only friend. She's been heartbroken."

"Poor kiddy," said the slaughterer. "It's dreadful how some people neglect their children."

"It's not quite like that. You don't understand," Matthew said. "Now, if you will excuse me, I must go and look at my rat. I noticed his coat was standing on end, which is a sign of ill health. He had a terrible night in Rugby."

I didn't want anyone to feel sorry for me. I didn't feel sorry for myself, for I knew my mother would come back. So when, as Matthew spoke of Rex, I witnessed the look of astonishment on the slaughterer's face, I found myself laughing. What a bizarre trio we must seem, I thought! "We're going to retrain him," I said, loud and clear, and then I told the slaughterer the story of Cassidy's life so far as we knew it.

"You've got a job on your hands, then," he said. "He's been conditioned you see."

"Well, what's the next move?" asked Penelope, taking off her glasses and smiling her telly smile. "Do we buy him back from you or what?"

"Haven't I seen you before somewhere? Excuse me asking, but aren't you Penelope . . .?" Recognition slowly dawned on the slaughterer's face.

"Penelope Randall, that's right," she smiled. "The dark glasses fooled you."

"Very pleased to meet you."

"Thank you," Penelope said. "Now what about it?"

"Well, as it happens, I've got a truck going in your direction this afternoon to fetch a load of cattle, so I'll drop the pony off, and Mr. Smithers must hand back the hundred pounds I paid him or I'll call in the police."

"We shall have to tell Sir Stanley," Penelope said.

"Well, it will be up to him to decide whether he wants a charge made against his groom," the slaughterer said. "Sometimes it's best to keep things out of court."

"Are you sure that's all right? I mean that you can transport him?" I asked. "Is it going to be a bother?"

"Listen, I don't want stolen property here a moment longer than's necessary. Right? Now you give me your exact address and you'll have him back sometime between four and five, so let's see a happy little smile on your face." The slaughterer patted me on the shoulder and, feeling like a child of six, I wondered whether my behaviour and lack of education warranted such treatment.

Matthew came back. "The rat's fine, gobbling the rest of that chocolate we bought."

"Come to the office and write the address down, Madam, please," the man said, "and while you're doing that I wonder whether I could ask you a little favour?"

"Of course," Penelope said.

"Just a little autograph for my daughter. She would be thrilled to bits, she has often seen you on telly."

"A pleasure," Penelope replied. "I'll give you three and then she can pass some on to her friends."

"Happier now?" she asked me a few minutes later, as we sped homewards.

"Oh yes, and thank you for everything. Thank you very much indeed," I said. "But please, please don't think I'm living a miserable life with Patsy. My mother will soon be home I'm sure. And my mother is wonderful. You'll love her when you meet her."

"Yes, I understand," Penelope said. "Only you do look rather forlorn sometimes, but the very fact that you can talk about it shows that you're weathering the storm very well. It's the people who can't articulate—excuse an awful word—that one must worry about."

"My mother and I talk about everything," I said firmly, and yet I knew as I spoke that I was telling a lie, for she had never told me about my grandparents or the sad parts of her own childhood. She had edited everything, so that I only knew about the happy times, never the bad ones. And my mother's marriage? What did I know of that, apart from the fact that she found living in the Soviet Union difficult?

"Where's the pony going to go?" asked Matthew. "I mean we can't put him in the field or Smithers might take him away to the Hunt. We must hide him."

"Our shed? Yes, what fun!" cried Penelope. "I can just see that sweet little face looking out."

"It's rather small," Matthew objected, "and only six feet high. You know that Meredith always hits his head. And what about the wheelbarrow and spades and forks and things."

"Move them out," replied Penelope promptly. "Look, where there's a will there's a way. That's our very next job. All hands to the wheel. We'll clean the place out. It will be super to have a pony at the bottom of the garden."

"But won't we have stolen him?" I asked.

"Not if we write post haste to Sir Stanley tonight informing him of the situation."

"But we haven't got his address in Corfu, and I don't trust that housekeeper to forward letters," I argued.

"Sir Sanley is a banker," Penelope said. "A very important banker. I shall write care of his London office and phone his secretary to make sure the letter is forwarded."

"Can you drive a little faster, Rex is shivering," Matthew begged. "I hope he didn't get a chill or pick up some virus last night."

"He ate the chocolate so he can't be all that ill," Penelope said, accelerating. "The spades and forks can go in the scullery and the wheelbarrow must sleep out."

"And bedding?" asked Matthew.

"Won't peat do? You know I got a couple of sacks for the garden. Well, they'll be all the more effective with a bit of horse dung mixed in."

"Penelope, you're a genius," said Matthew. "There's only one thing."

"And what's that?"

"Are you sure you are really sensible to send me to that expensive boarding school? I mean O-Levels aren't everything. And I can't say I took to the headmaster. And I'm simply not going to leave Rex behind, and you're being mean to Tao. The whole thing is the stupidest idea, and I think you're doing it just to get rid of me . . ."

"Oh darling!" said Penelope. "Please!"

I froze. I swear my blood turned cold, as suddenly I realized to some degree how much Matthew meant to me. Life with Patsy without his companionship would be unbearable, even with Cassidy to retrain. The days would be empty.

"Boarding school?" my voice said, sounding far away, different.

"Yes," said Matthew with some bitterness. "My glandular fever has put me back."

"It isn't just that," cut in Penelope. "The comprehensive just doesn't push you enough. It's your future we are thinking about, darling. Nowadays nobody gets anywhere without a decent education."

"As well as the fact that you will both be on location in Mexico this winter," added Matthew. "And you want me out of the way."

"We want you well cared for. You can't stay at the cottage alone. That arrangement is most unsatisfactory," said Penelope, slowing down to touch his knee with motherly affection.

"Please hurry," urged Matthew frowning. "I want to give Rex a drink. I think he may be thirsty."

"And who will look after him?" I asked, finding my voice at last.

"I don't know. Would you, Katie? Could you?"

"Oh Matthew, I would if possible, but I don't know where I shall be. I don't know anything until my mother comes back. Perhaps she said something in that letter we lost. I wish someone had been good enough to hand it in to Lost Property. Patsy drew a blank."

91

"How's the reading?" said Penelope, sounding glad to change the subject.

"He says I'm not dis, dis, whatever it is."

"Dyslexic," said Penelope. "The teacher you mean."

"Yes, that's right. It's just that I've changed schools too often and never gained any self confidence or continuity. He says I will soon learn."

"Just what I thought!" cried Penelope. "Good for you! You are so articulate, too. You use such long words. A wonderful vocabulary for your age."

"He says I will learn to read my name this evening. It's just a matter of hard work and concentration. But, Matthew, I will certainly look after Rex during term time if I have a home; I should love to. But I don't think we could take him into lodgings. I don't think landladies and house owners like rats," I said.

"They're so ignorant," complained Matthew. "Prejudiced!"

Then we were turning into the Trumpingtons' little drive.

"Now to work," cried Penelope. "Katie. You help me clear out the shed while Matthew fetches the peat."

"It looks dreadfully small," I said.

"I must see to Rex first," insisted Matthew, hurrying indoors with the rat on his shoulder.

CHAPTER TWELVE

A POSTCARD FROM ROUMANIA

Cassidy was very excited when he arrived. He arched his neck and carried his tail as though he was an Arab, and blew noisily through distended nostrils. But he didn't like the shed much and kept pawing the ground. He wanted a door to look over.

"Matthew must saw it in half tomorrow, and I'll go to the ironmongers and buy two bolts and a hook to hold back the top half," Penelope said. "We'll turn the shed into a loose box."

We had no hay, but fortunately the grass at the end of

the Trumpingtons' little orchard was long. Matthew and I cut Cassidy armfuls with a grass hook, which he ate greedily between uttering loud neighs that seemed to carry for miles.

"I only hope the wicked Smithers doesn't hear," said Penelope with a smile. "Goodness, it has been quite a day. Who's for a drink? A Campari soda for me, please Matthew. What about you, Katie?"

"My lesson! My bus goes in ten minutes," I said. "And I ought to brush my hair."

"Yes, you must look worth saving from illiteracy!" said Penelope. "Matthew, a drink darling. I am totally exhausted."

"Rex doesn't seem to want the sunflower seeds. I hope he's all right," her son answered, a frown bringing his brows together above his nose. "Yes, all right, a Campari." He sighed.

"Is there anything I can buy for Rex in Solihull?" I asked. "I expect some newsagents will still be open."

But Matthew said no, thank you, so I ran off at once to Patsy's place and, after tidying myself up, caught the bus with about one second to spare. I should have been happy now that Cassidy was saved but, instead, I felt drained, as though I had experienced too much emotion in too short a space of time. Also a name was playing havoc in the back of my mind, prodding my memory, digging in my brain's filing system. SMITHERS. I didn't see it in letters, of course, as you might have done, but I heard it as a sound— Smithers. Then, as the bus rounded a corner, Patsy's voice spoke from the deeper recesses of my brain. It was bright and cheerful, as Patsy's voice always is, except when she is very angry or very depressed. It said: "Yes, and farmed you out with a lovely fat woman, called Mrs. Smithers, whom you adored."

"Could that foster mother have been that crook's wife?" I asked myself wildly. "Could that groom have bounced me on his knee, while his fat wife made the tea?" The thought seemed almost too much to bear at the end of a long day, for in my mind Mr. Smithers had swiftly become an arch villain, a man without goodness or compassion. Perhaps his wife was different, I told myself. Women sometimes made foolish or disastrous marriages. The bus came to a halt and I stepped off and walked in a sort of trance to the semi-detached, 'thirties house in which my tutor lived.

"You look anxious," he said on opening the door to my knock. "Everything all right?"

"Oh fine, thank you," I replied.

"Heard from your mother?"

"Not yet, but I soon will."

"Right, well come through and let's begin then, or would you like a cup of coffee or something first?"

"Coffee, yes please," I said, after a pause. "It's been a hectic day."

"What happened then?" asked the teacher, going through into the kitchen to put on a kettle.

"Oh, nothing much," I said.

To my surprise, despite my tiredness, the lesson proved very profitable and, at last, some words seemed to take shape. We worked for twenty minutes and then took a break for ten minutes while my teacher chatted to me, then we continued for another concentrated twenty minutes, and so on for a total of two hours. Then it was time for me to catch my bus back.

"You're doing very well," he said, patting me on the shoulder. "I'm very pleased with you, but I wonder whether you need more help to sort out your life in general. It seems to me that you have a lot of secret worries. I feel that you are holding things back."

"You mean, a doctor, a psychologist?" I asked suspiciously.

"You don't miss a trick, do you?" He laughed. "It beats me how you know about these things when you can't read."

"My mother," I said. "My mother doesn't want me to see a psychologist. We've been through that before, she and I. I won't see anyone else until she's back."

"All right," he said. "All right, Katie, don't get worked up. We won't make you do anything. Just trust us."

He looked deep into my face, his grey eyes full of concern; but I only thought about his moustache, wishing he would shave it off. He was too young, I thought, to take on the appearance of a walrus. The beastly, drooping thing contradicted the youthfulness of his eyes. He could be quite handsome, but . . .

"I don't get worked up," I said angrily, at last. "I learn a great deal from television."

"Don't get me wrong," my teacher said, squeezing my shoulder reassuringly. "We are all on your side. I think you are very gifted. So does my wife—from what I tell her."

"It's not much use if one can't read or write," I said.

"Agreed! Your bus . . ." he said, glancing at his digital watch. "You'll miss it if you don't run. See you tomorrow. And don't forget the homework."

Patsy had returned when I got back. "I still don't know what to do about Madeira," she said.

"I should book it. My mother must be back soon," I said. "She wouldn't leave me more than a month or two. I know she wouldn't, not unless she's met with an accident."

"Or the Soviets won't let her out."

"Well, perhaps I could find someone to foster me. What about Mrs. Smithers?" I asked.

"Oh, she moved away."

"To Leconfield Stud?"

"I don't know. Besides, a woman who loves babies doesn't necessarily know how to cope with adolescents."

"Am I an adolescent?"

"Afraid so," said Patsy, beginning to cut up a lettuce. "Deal with those tomatoes, would you? How was the lesson?"

"Fine," I said. "Did Mrs. Smithers like horses? I mean was she married to a groom?"

"I believe she was. Now, could you open that tin of sweet corn? I think we'll have rye bread tonight. It's full of vitamin B."

"Sir Stanley has a groom called Smithers," I said, tipping the corn into a pottery dish.

"That could be. Do you want to visit your old friend? It would be a kind thought. But Smithers is a common name. It could be a different couple."

"I don't know what to say." I said.

95

"Sometimes, it's better not to revisit the past," remarked Patsy spreading butter thinly on the bread. "Mix a dressing for the salad, please: sunflower oil, wine vinegar, paprika, French mustard, salt and a pinch of brown sugar."

"Rex isn't very well," I said. "We found him, but his coat is standing up."

"I expect he's getting old," Patsy said. "Rats only live three or four years, I think."

"Matthew has to go to boarding school," I added, reaching for the bottle of vinegar.

"Well, he certainly needs to go somewhere. He hardly seemed to go to the local place at all. It was ridiculous, leaving him on his own like that. It didn't give the school a chance."

"He doesn't know what to do with Rex. I was wondering . . ."

"Not here, no. I won't have a rat, that's flat. Anyway, what about Felix?"

"He's so sweet with his little brown cape; it's like a monk's cowl, and his eyes, the intelligence . . ."

"Not another word. The answer is no. Not so much vinegar, for goodness sake!"

I wanted to tell Patsy about Cassidy, but all through supper she talked about my future, my education. She knew of a wonderful Quaker school, which took intelligent but backward children, and concentrated on drama, art and music. She had made enquiries. There was a place available. It was now only a question of money. If my mother was really penniless, I might get a bursary or some foundation scholarship.

"But Mummy is dead against boarding schools," I said. "She doesn't want me moulded. She wants me to be her daughter."

"Possessiveness can be a form of selfishness," said Patsy crisply.

After supper I went to see Cassidy and to watch television with Matthew. The pony was quieter, although still annoyed at being shut in the dark.

"I expect he has always slept under the stars," I said.

"Except when it rained or snowed. You're a hopeless

romantic, you know Katie, the stars don't always shine," said Matthew. "And he was probably brought in the night before a rodeo. Penelope is trying to find out whether she can lay her hands on a stunt rider to cure him."

"A stunt rider?"

"You know: famous film stars don't risk their lives on dangerous feats. The great cowboys in Westerns have stunt riders to do the rodeo riding. Now if we could find one of those over here, he could stick on Cassidy's back and cure him."

"But does she know any stunt riders?" I asked.

"No, but she's going to ring around tomorrow. You know, I never thought I could become fond of ponies, but that little thing in the shed is rather nice isn't he? He whinnies whenever he hears my footsteps, and he's addicted to Polos."

"And his eyes are so bright, and his little ears so sharp," I added. "And he loves us. He needs human company."

"Oh, we know you are besotted," said Matthew with a laugh. "Aren't you tired? We are. We're going to bed."

"The time?" I asked.

"Ten o'clock."

"Me, too, then," I said. "I didn't realize it was that late."

But I wasn't tired. Or, anyway, I couldn't sleep. My mind was on Mrs. Smithers. How could I bear to be the girl that sent her husband to court, when she had loved me when I was a lonely baby with a mother all day at work? The question tormented me, and yet I told myself over and over again that it was senseless to worry before I knew for certain whether Smithers the groom was husband of the woman who had cared for me. "It might never happen," I kept telling myself, but still the idea possessed me and drove all hope of sleep away, so that when morning came I was pale with red-rimmed eyes and dark shadows.

"You look as though you've spent a night on the tiles," said Patsy, as she ate her last mouthful of toast and marmalade.

"What does that mean?"

"Oh, never mind, it isn't exactly apt for your

generation," she said. "I must rush. If the shop opens late I shall lose customers."

After she had gone, a postcard arrived with a picture of a long sandy beach, bathers and a blue sky. The stamp was unfamiliar and the writing was my mother's. I could actually read "Katie" and "Mummy". I ate a bowl of cereal and dashed round to the Trumpingtons.

"News," I cried. "Look at this."

Penelope was in her dressing-gown; her lovely golden hair tangled but her face glowing. "Matthew is still in bed," she told me. "Do you think he's very upset about boarding school?"

"Yes, dreadfully. I would be too." I handed her the postcard.

"It's from Roumania," she said slowly, "from a Black Sea resort and it says: 'Having a marvellous time, but looking forward to seeing you again, darling. We both send our love, and are brown from sea and sun. Look after yourself, Katie, I miss you dreadfully. Love to Patsy, Mummy.'"

"Oh," I mused.

"She must mean that your father is out of the Soviet Union. Perhaps he will defect from Roumania. Perhaps there's a plot and she'll bring him back after all," said Penelope, sounding excited. "I say, it is quite a drama, isn't it?"

Suddenly I was afraid of meeting my father.

"I must get on with my reading," I said. "He told me to study. He'll be amazed if he finds I can't read. After all, I'm going to be fourteen soon. I mean, people used to leave school at fourteen."

"Well, there you are. That's given you something to think about," smiled Penelope. "Now, if you don't mind, Katie darling, I'm going to have my bath. I've written to Sir Stanley, but I have yet to phone his secretary. Meanwhile, could you feed the poor pony? He's been whinnying ever since six o'clock this morning."

"Of course," I said at once, mortified that I might have been a nuisance appearing so early and, as though in answer, Cassidy pawed the ground in his shed and gave a great bellow of welcome or despair.

CHAPTER THIRTEEN

A HORRIBLE INTERVIEW

"You're never the little Russian baby!" exclaimed Mrs. Smithers, on the doorstep, smiling above her double chin and patting me with her pudgy hands. "Such a pretty little mite you were, with those wonderful blue eyes, a determined little beggar, too. Crawl!—I've never seen anything like it. You got into everything, once you found you could move around."

"You're disappointed in me now, then?" I asked, all too ready to face the worst and torture myself with it afterwards.

"No, no, but a thirteen-year-old is very different from a mite of five to ten months, isn't she? It stands to reason. But you were a bonnie baby, and I was that proud of you. You had such a wide little face. You were different from the others and, at the clinic, I used to say! "Ah, but this one is from the wild steppes of Russia, and has a Papa with a big black beard and snow on his boots!" I never failed to raise a laugh, and everyone would come to look at you then, as though you were something special. Of course your mother usually had you back with her at night. I was more a nanny than a foster parent."

"Well, it's great to meet up again," I said politely, with a sinking heart and little enthusiasm.

"Come in, sit down, have a cup of tea," urged Mrs. Smithers. "George will be back directly and that excited to see you again. He used to call you Rusky. And what happened to the marriage? Did they come together again? I've often wondered."

I explained about my mother being in Eastern Europe, seeing my father, and that I didn't know what the result would be.

"They may send for you," said Mrs. Smithers, pouring hot water over the tea leaves. "Would you like to go? Would you like to live there?"

I said that I didn't know, but my mother had said I

would find the education excellent, but the way of life constricting.

"Yes, your mother always spoke her mind," Mrs. Smithers said, while I looked at the door, afraid that George would come in and recognize me. I cleared my throat, then gulped.

"Look, I've got something horrible to tell you," I whispered. "Something you don't want to hear."

"Your mother's never been and died!" exclaimed Mrs. Smithers, pouring out tea.

"No, I've told you, she's in Eastern Europe."

"Has she disowned you then? Are you abandoned? Don't say that! Mind you I would never put anything past your mother. A lovely girl, but wild. She seemed to move from one crisis to another. Gone back to Russia and left you all on your little own with Mrs. Cooper, has she? Oh, the wicked girl!"

"No, no, it's about the pony, Sir Stanley's pony," I began again.

"Been destroyed you mean. Well, it had to come. The animal was dangerous. There's no point in feeding a useless animal, is there? He broke plenty of bones, and that sort's no good to man nor beast. A bullet in the head is the only answer. The same with murderers. They should hang. I want capital punishment back, and birching. Violence must be repaid with violence. It's the only way. And everyone, man and beast, should earn his living."

"No, no. The pony is alive," I said, looking round the little room, taking in the worn mats on the new, garishly patterned linoleum, the scarred table, the shabby chair and the smarter armchair, covered in a cheap imitation of chintz, in which Mrs. Smithers now sat, fat and complacent, her face sinking into its chins, one hand stirring with a spoon the milky tea in a chipped cup.

"He's dead, went to the kennels yesterday or was it the day before?" she insisted.

"I can't explain," I said at last.

"No, I understand, dear. I know, you were fond of the little pony; it's only natural, especially if your mother's left you on your own again. Now drink your tea before it gets cold and don't upset yourself. Would you like a biscuit? You always fancied a nibble at the Rich Tea variety when you were tiny, a greedy little monkey you were! And you had two little dimples, but they've gone now. You've a sad face now, not surprising in the circumstances."

"Please tell your husband that we fetched the pony from the horse slaughterer's and that he must give the money back," I said. "Someone is going to tell Sir Stanley what your husband has done." I stood up. I was trembling. "It was a lovely cup of tea, and thank you, thank you for everything; thank you for looking after me when I was little. I'm sorry to bring bad news."

"I don't know what you are talking about," said Mrs. Smithers, bridling, her face suddenly hard. "It's up to my husband to dispose of a carcass as he thinks fit. Grooms have perks you know the same as everyone else. Farm workers have milk, miners have coal, company directors have cars, bankers have cheap loans, egg sorters, cracked eggs. It's only fair. Everyone has to make a bit of money on the side to survive these days. Why even gardeners sell off the thinnings when they thin out the cabbages."

"I'm sorry," I said, edging towards the door. "I just wanted to tell you I didn't want that to happen. I just wanted to save Cassidy, and now to warn you both."

"You're as cunning as your mother then, no gratitude for all I did for you, and only half paid I was. Why, the little bit she gave me hardly covered the cost of the porridge and the rusks."

"I'm sorry," I said again, blushing. "When we started to look for Cassidy we didn't know he had been sold for meat, honestly we did not."

"You're blushing," she said, following me close to the door, "that means you're telling lies. Your conscience isn't clear. You're trying to ruin a working man who took you into his home when your mother was penniless."

In the full light of the morning sun, I saw how ugly she was; soft and overblown with a shapeless nose, and I wondered suddenly how I could have loved her. I imagined myself on her lap, pressed against her sagging breasts.

"You were happier then," I said.

"What do you mean?"

"Thirteen years ago," I said, and saw for an instant a different light in her eyes as she reached backwards for some memory, some joy which had made her life better.

"It's true," she said. "But it's no business of yours."

"I'll do everything I can to help, everything," I cried, near tears, "but the letter has gone to Sir Stanley, and I can't stop that."

"Go on, then," she said. "Go and don't come back. I'd rather remember you as you were, just an innocent little mite, with two lovely dimples."

As I walked back across the park, I refused to be downcast. I told myself that my mother was bound to be home in time for my birthday, which was in ten days' time. In all my life she had never forgotten that day. And if she was in Roumania she was already halfway back. She would sort things out, I thought. She must. And perhaps I would have a father who would manage things, buy a house, drive a car, dig the garden, do all the things other fathers did. Even Russian fathers must know how to manage the everyday things of life, I told myself. He would be a chess player, I decided, amusing and sad in turns. But strong, a man who could cut down trees with one blow, and remind my mother of all the things she usually forgot. Everything was now going to get better. I cared not a jot for Mrs. Smithers because of the horrible things she had said about my mother, whom I loved more than anyone else in the world, more than Cassidy or Matthew, I told myself—well, at the moment, anyway. I hated to think of myself being cuddled by that woman, fed from a bottle, handed rusks, pushed to the clinic, having my little hands sponged. I felt she might have tainted me.

I went back to the Trumpingtons and took Cassidy for a walk down the lanes. Tao barked miserably from the window, but there was no sign of Matthew or Penelope. I wondered whether Patsy would remember my birthday if my mother's return was delayed. It would be awful to wake up and find not a single present awaiting me. I wondered whether I should tell the Trumpingtons, so that at least I might have one parcel to open, but decided against doing so, because it might seem like begging.

I groomed Cassidy and pulled his black mane, until it

was about nine inches long, and washed his hoofs and tail. Then I mucked out the shed, which should have been my first job, and polished him with my bath towel until he shone like a beautiful conker or piece of furniture. While I worked I talked to him about my life and hopes, suggested that one day it was just possible that I might marry Matthew.

After a while Mrs. Carter arrived.

"So they've taken that rat to the vet," she said. "Left a message for me, and asked if you would walk the dog. How are you getting along, all right?"

"Oh yes," I said. "Just fine, thanks."

"Learning to read?"

"Yes, fine thanks."

"Mother coming back soon?"

"Yes."

"You'll be happy then."

"Yes, that's right."

"And now you've got the pony. That's nice, isn't it? Ever so nice for you. And the boy too. I never thought Matthew was that interested in girls, but then he's past fourteen and they start so early these days," said Mrs. Carter. "Well, it's almost twelve, and I must get on. It's my late morning today. I've been putting Mrs. Sims straight first, a proper muddle she gets in, seeing her sight's going. I'll just get you Tao's lead."

"Is the rat ill?"

"Must be! You don't take a fit animal to the vet, unless you're a nuisance."

"Only for vaccinations, that sort of thing," I said. "Matthew must be worried."

"Yes, he's dotty about that rat, can't stand rodents myself, never could," said Mrs. Carter. "And what's to happen when he goes away to school? There's no boarding kennels for rats. Here you are. Take care of the dog."

I took Tao along a footpath by the wheatfields. The corn was swollen now and turning golden, and here and there were poppies bright as blood, but beautiful in their delicacy amongst the straight stems of the wheat. Overhead a summer sun was partly obscured by white clouds thick as cotton wool. If Mother was flying now she would be above those clouds, I told myself, nearer the golden sun, tearing through a sea of deep blue, the clouds beneath her, a white bed, billowy, welcoming but, in the end, no more than vapour. I had never flown myself except as a baby, but my mother had described her many journeys to me in detail. My mother was a compulsive talker and often I was her only audience, and so I had learned much from her, since she had once been one of the world's travellers, a happy beaded person who hitch-hiked from country to country. And her views on every subject were numerous. She had no roots, no set ideas, few rules of life, although she treasured loyalty, friendship and absolute honesty, as well as courage. Just now I wanted her very badly.

I kept Tao on the lead, as I wasn't sure whether she would come when I called her, but she walked very well, without pulling, stopping now and then to sniff. As I turned back for home I forgot my mother and I wondered about the rat again, and then about Matthew. How deeply upset was he at the thought of boarding school? I could not see him fitting in to a fixed regime. His life had been so free to date and, in a way, he was too adult to stand a hearty boyish life where games were all important.

When I arrived back at the Trumpingtons' cottage, their car was still absent, but a cattle truck stood outside.

"A man has called for the pony," said Mrs. Carter opening the cottage door. "Taking him to the Hunt, as Sir Stanley Petworth ordered."

"Not Mr. Smithers?" I cried.

"What's that, pet?"

"Here." I dropped Tao's lead and ran round to the shed, in time to see the cattle truck driver putting a headcollar on Cassidy.

"No," I said. "No! You can't take that pony."

"What's that? I've come to the right place, haven't I? Here we are."

He pulled a grubby piece of paper from his pocket and read: "Mrs. Trumpington, Rose Cottage, Winchwood-in-Arden."

"Sir Stanley has almost certainly changed his plans by now," I said firmly.

"But his groom . . ."

"Not to be trusted," I replied, taking off the headcollar.

"But the call only came through an hour ago," objected the driver. "People don't change their minds that quickly. Besides Sir Stanley is said to be abroad."

"Exactly," I said. "That's why the order has been given so suddenly. Mr. Smithers wants the pony dead by the time Sir Stanley returns."

"But that was Sir Stanley's orders," argued the truck driver. "I've lived round these parts all my life. I know who's who in the horse world, see. I know the kennel huntsman, too, and I knew George Smithers when he was at Leconfield Stud. He says he'll be given the push, the sack, if that pony's not dead by the time Sir Stanley's daughter gets back."

I began to cry. I was ashamed, bitterly ashamed as the tears started to run out of my eyes, but I couldn't stop them. Suddenly I was very tired.

"He's such a lovely pony," I sobbed. "He's been such a friend to me. He means no harm. Look at his face, look!"

"Now don't take on," the man said. "He's not yours to keep. Is he? You haven't bought him."

"That doesn't make any difference," I said, rubbing my eyes with my fists. "Ownership doesn't mean much when it comes to cruelty."

"He won't feel anything. Mr. Dawson is expert with a humane killer. It will be all over before he knows what's happening."

"He'll be dead," I wailed, running my hands through Cassidy's mane.

"But he's no good to anyone," the driver said, looking at me kindly, almost imploringly.

I leaned against the door. "You'll have to drag me away," I said, "and then I shall lie in front of your truck, like the suffragettes. No one has ever taken the trouble to find out why he bucks. You have condemned him to death without a fair trial."

Suddenly I felt very calm and at least twenty years old. I straightened my back and felt, after all, that I might be a heroine, and then I saw that the man was weakening.

"So please go away," I said.

"I'll have to tell Mr. Smithers."

"Yes."

My trembling had stopped; my tear ducts dried up; my face felt set like a statue's, immovable, but when the man had gone, when the truck's rumbling and rattle had disappeared in the distance, cold shivers ran down my spine and the old wrung-out-mop feeling returned.

"Has he gone? Didn't he take the pony, pet?" asked Mrs. Carter, leaning out of a window.

"Yes, no," I said.

"You look white. Come in, I'll make you some coffee. You don't eat enough. Mrs. Cooper doesn't leave you enough. What's a sandwich to a growing girl? Too much health food."

I was sitting in the kitchen with Tao's head on my knee with Mrs. Carter kindly fussing round me when the Trumpingtons returned.

"The vet gave him a massive injection of penicillin. It hurt terribly," said Matthew coming in with Rex in his cupped hands. "The poor little thing grimaced. He screwed up his face just like a human being and squealed as the needle went in. Rats are terribly hard to inject, because they're all muscle and bone."

"What is it?" I asked.

"He doesn't know. Maybe a virus or infection or both," said Matthew. "I wish I had never taken him to Rugby."

"You look all in. What's happened?" asked Penelope. "Did you get our message? Did you take Tao for a walk? Did you mind us asking?"

"She's had a shock, poor girl," said Mrs. Carter.

"Something about her mother? Oh darling, I am so sorry," cried Penelope. "I have been so afraid that something might go wrong."

"A man came for the pony," said Mrs. Carter in tones of great solemnity.

"For Cassidy?"

"Just let me have a little more coffee. Let me get my breath back, and then I'll explain," I said. "I sent him off, but he'll probably return with Smithers."

"So please go away," I said.
"I'll have to tell Mr Smithers
"Yes

CHAPTER FOURTEEN

AN UNWANTED CALLER

During the afternoon I took Cassidy to graze in the Trumpingtons' little orchard, while Matthew tested my reading. He had made special cards for me on which he had written words in careful Roman script. *Penelope, Cassidy, Matthew, Tao, Rex, Rat, Cat, Pony, Father, Groom* and *Russia.* These were the words he thought I would find most useful during the next few weeks. Every now and then he flashed a card in front of me, so that I could call out what it said. Now that I had begun official lessons, I seemed to be learning very quickly and it wasn't long before I had mastered all eleven cards.

"It is all a matter of self confidence," Matthew assured me. "Do try to read the newspapers or buy a comic. Keep practising. I want you to write to me when I'm at boarding school, and to read my replies. I couldn't bear other people to read them to you."

"You will have to write very simply and very large at first," I told him. "I bet you'll do well."

"I'm going at the wrong age. Most people go at eleven or thirteen, not almost fifteen. So I shall find it hard to make friends."

"You're looking on the black side," I said. "You might be made head boy. You don't know what fate has in store for you!"

"Oh, you're nuts," cried Matthew in despair. "Me, head boy! I can't even play cricket."

"Brains," I said, tapping my forehead.

"Brains don't count at that sort of school," insisted Matthew.

"Self confidence," I said, with a mocking smile.

Then Tao barked and ran towards the front gate, her tail curled tightly and her hackles up.

"It's him. I feel it in my bones," I said.

"Who? Your bones are often wrong."

"Smithers!"

"Yes, you're actually right," said Matthew in astonishment. "Bold as brass!"

Mr. Smithers had a leather headcollar in his hand, and a grim expression on his red face. His blue eyes looked as cold as the blade of a carving knife poised to cut a joint, and his empty fist was clenched so tight that the knuckles shone white.

"Here we go!" said Matthew with a nervous little laugh. "Hold the pony tight, Katie. Don't give him an inch."

The man stopped. He looked us both up and down.

"Damned interfering kids!" he said. "Your sort should be in detention centres, stealing someone else's pony."

"It's you who stole," said Matthew, standing straight and firm right in the groom's path.

"Do you want me to knock you down, son?" asked Smithers, his eyes turning fierce now like little flames from lighted methylated spirits.

"Go ahead," said Matthew. "Have a go!"

"I've come to take back my employer's pony, and no one is going to stop me," Smithers growled.

"We are, because you sold him for a hundred pounds, and he wasn't yours to sell. You wanted him dead, and money in your pocket." Matthew said.

"That's none of your business. If this silly Russian kid hadn't taken it into her head to make a pet of him, the pony would have been spared until the winter. It was in her interest that Sir Stanley decided to have him put down this month."

"She's not a silly Russian kid. She's half English and a damned sight more intelligent than you!" cried Matthew.

"I won't have any cheek from a boy like you," said Smithers, advancing to push Matthew to one side, and then in a flash grabbing the rope with which I held the peacefully grazing Cassidy. "And if you ask me, her mother was never married to that Russian at all."

"Oh yes, she was," I shouted. "I've seen the certificate. She had to send it to the Embassy for a visa or something. I was with her when it was xeroxed. She waved it at me."

Matthew extracted himself from the bush in which the groom had pushed him. "We'll have you for slander," he cried. "My mother knows about slander. Give back that pony!" he grappled with the groom, but was soon sent flying again, while I fared little better.

"You kill the pony and I shall kill you!" I shouted idiotically, my thoughts now horribly out of control.

"After all my wife did for you!" exclaimed the groom. "Selfish little beggar, but then what can you expect with a mother like that, bad blood always will out."

Then Matthew hit the groom on the jaw with his fist, but the man was tough as wood it seemed, and Matthew's hand hurt so much afterwards that he was forced to pause and clasp it to his chest.

Meanwhile Smithers was down the path and almost at the gate, pushing me roughly aside. "He's bionic or something!" Matthew gasped. "He doesn't feel."

"Trip him with your foot!" I cried, tugging at the groom's trousers, trying to pull him back. Then suddenly, miraculously, Smithers stopped; the pony snorted, and a deep growl brought us both to a standstill. Tao was in the gateway. Dog-like she had understood our desperation and, after a moment, knew that the man was taking something that belonged to her owners. Her hackles were up again, her lovely teeth gleamed white against the mulberry colour of her jaws. Cassidy started to back away.

"Whoa there, come on!" shouted the groom, tugging at the rope. "Get down dog, get back!" He raised a foot as though to kick the chow and, in an instant, Tao had sunk her teeth into that leg. With a yell of pain, Smithers dropped the rope and Cassidy trotted back up the garden, and began to graze again in the orchard.

"Leave him!" commanded Matthew. "Enough, Tao!"

The chow relaxed her jaws, and the back door opened to reveal Penelope, beautiful in a long flowered skirt and glorious silk shirt.

"What on earth is happening? My dear man, you're bleeding!"

"This is Smithers, Mr. Smithers," Matthew explained. "He came to take Cassidy away to send him to the Hunt or to sell or something, and Tao stopped him."

"We'd better bathe that leg," Penelope said. "It looks nasty."

"I'll have the police after you for this, for assault," the man said.

"Well, let's clean your leg first or you might suffer blood poisoning. Come on in, and have a cup of tea while I find some antiseptic. Put the kettle on, Matthew. Or would you prefer whisky?" Penelope sounded incredibly calm and in control.

Deflated, the groom hobbled into the Trumpingtons' pine kitchen, sat on a chair and put his head in his hands.

"Do you want to speak to Sir Stanley?" asked Penelope very perkily.

"Madam, you know that he's in Corfu," the groom said, his face screwed up in pain.

"No, not today. I spoke to his secretary this morning, and she told me that he left the island last night to do a spot of business in Athens. She gave me a telephone number to ring if needed. Arabella and her mother are still in Corfu, of course, but he's available. I am used to making long-distance calls. My husband is away so much."

The man whitened then.

"You spoke to his secretary?" he said, in a voice hardly above a whisper.

"Yes, I put her in the picture," said Penelope brightly. "Now come on let's get that trouser leg up. Oh, not too bad! A couple of punctures, might be wise to have a penicillin injection, just in case, dogs being dogs."

"I'll have that dog put down. He's not safe. He's dangerous, might bite a kiddy," the groom said.

"No, no. You were a trespasser who refused to leave when asked," Penelope said, soothingly. "You haven't a hope. Usually she's the most gentle of beasts. In fact, she has surprised us all today."

"She's a wonder dog," said Matthew kneeling to caress the chow.

"I'll run you back in the car," offered Penelope, after she had bathed the two punctures, and put on antiseptic ointment and sticking plasters.

"I'll drive myself. I've got a car outside," said Mr. Smithers. And then we knew that we had won.

"Better look after Cassidy, Katie," Penelope said. "The

fence at the bottom of the garden isn't exactly pony proof. We don't want to lose him."

Later that evening, when I went for my reading lesson, the tutor put me through a verbal intelligence test, having explained the importance of looking for a common factor when trying to answer the questions. With his help, I managed for the first time in my life to complete the examination, and I was so surprised and pleased that I said: "You know, I think this is one of the best days of my life," and then I told him all about Cassidy. I talked for so long that I missed my bus, but my tutor said it didn't matter. He would drive me back, and then he stayed for a cup of coffee and a chat with Patsy. He said some rather nice things about me which I won't repeat, and suddenly I began to feel that a whole new world was opening up. I thought how marvellous it would be when I could read like other children, when I could look things up in books, and use encyclopædias and not be at the bottom of the class.

"It all depends on her wretched mother," Patsy said. "A charming, pretty girl but vague and wayward. If only she can be persuaded to stay in one place for a few years to give the poor child some stability, then I think we might see some rapid progress. Katie's father is an engineer of some talent, I believe, and in many ways she's very advanced for thirteen but, in a technical sense, chronically backward."

"You may be right. Boarding school might be the answer," my tutor said.

Then, not wanting to eavesdrop and affronted at being called a child, I went off to visit Cassidy. The Trumpingtons had fixed the door with a chain and padlock so I could not enter the shed and was forced to talk to my friend through a crack in the wood. He whinnied softly in reply, and I could feel the sweet, grassy warmness of his breath.

"You're safe now," I said. "For the time being at any rate. But do kick Smithers if he comes again. I hate him, you see, for what he has done to you for filthy money and for what he has said about Mummy. I have never hated anyone so much in my life." As I spoke I seemed to feel my hatred welling up inside me.

When I returned to the lodge I found Patsy showing my tutor a snapshot of my mother.

"I say, she's quite a girl, isn't she? Smashing," the man said.

"But you see sadly her childhood was broken by that appalling car smash. She hardly knew her parents," Patsy said. "She worships Katie, of course, but knows nothing about bringing up children. She's a gypsy at heart. A woman of no fixed address. She borrowed the return fare to Moscow."

CHAPTER FIFTEEN

A SAD DAY

I must have slept well, because I wakened with an over-whelming sense of happiness and well-being. My room was flooded with sunlight, for I had not drawn the curtains. The scent of roses and yellow honeysuckle came in through the open window and a small plane droned lazily overhead. Exhausted no doubt by their dawn chorus, the birds were silent, but I could hear in the distance the mooing of cows and the miaowing of Felix as he came back from some nocturnal hunting trip.

My bones told me again that my mother would soon return, and I wanted now, quite desperately, to see the owner of that deep foreign voice who had asked me to be a good girl. "My father," I said aloud. "My Russian father." Most people had fathers, but few in England possessed Russian fathers. I was going to be different, yes respectably different, and the thought pleased me, and husbands, I thought, usually insisted on permanent homes.

I could hear Patsy downstairs preparing her breakfast. Longing to get up, I waited tactfully until she had gone. After all, I had become now an unwanted guest, so I must do everything in my power to fit in. But now that we had saved Cassidy and my mother was safely in Roumania, I was not going to allow anything to depress me, not even the thought of Matthew at boarding school, because he was going to write to me, and soon I would be able to write back and, in the circumstances, this seemed a wonderful and romantic way in which to continue our friendship. In addition there was the chance that I might be able to look after Rex for him, if my mother was going to plump for a more settled existence. Certainly she would welcome the little rat. She was indeed a "conservationist", who had campaigned against the culling of seals, battery hen houses, the destruction of bird sanctuaries, the intensive rearing of calves for veal, and much else besides. And if my father was again in love with my mother, he would of course agree to everything she wanted.

Presently I got out of bed and fetched an ancient reading book Patsy had found in an antique chest of drawers she had brought from a sick old lady. It was called *Crown Infant Reader No. 1* and the first story began: "I am up on my ox," and to my astonishment I read this without really concentrating and then, thinking about what the sentence meant, I burst out laughing. "Whoever gets up on an ox?" I asked myself.

Half an hour later I was dressed and knocking on the Trumpingtons' door. Penelope came sleepy-eyed.

"Sorry, did I get you out of bed?" I asked, thinking only of Cassidy who was banging in the shed with his hoofs and whinnying.

"Oh yes, you want the padlock key. Wait a moment. No, I needed waking up. I've work to do, don't worry."

Penelope was, I thought as she handed me the key, one of the kindest people in the world. Famous and nice, and never cross, not with me, anyway.

I grazed Cassidy in the orchard for a while, and then Matthew came out, wearing jeans and a ragged old shirt. His hair was unbrushed and his face drawn, so that his nose looked larger than usual, and his eyes even more brilliant beneath their thick beautifully arched brows.

"Rex is dead," he said, fetching a spade.

"Oh no!" I cried, after a moment's pause while the news sank in. "Why, how, what happened?"

"He came downstairs in the evening when we were watching television. It was so odd, because he's never done that before. He came making little crooning noises, and he sat on my shoulder pressing himself against my face. He was trying to tell me something, probably about how ill he felt. But I thought he was hungry. I fetched him sunflower seeds, and he held those in his little pink paws, but didn't actually eat them. I should have realized that he was too weak to bite hard. I should have made him gruel or something. He didn't want to leave me, so I sat up in bed with him on my knee stroking him. He was frightened. He's never been frightened before, and his eyes sort of implored me." Matthew paused. He ran a hand through his untidy hair and blinked hard. "I should have taken him to the vet, but I didn't think he was dangerously ill, and I didn't want to bother someone in the middle of the night. I thought this morning would do. But then, at about two o'clock this morning, Rex suddenly jumped out of my arms, ran a few paces across the floor and fell dead, dead."

"Oh Matthew," I began. "I'm so sorry . . ."

"No, please don't say anything. He was only a rat, and if I hadn't taken him he would have been killed when a baby. There's nothing to be done now. It's too late. You once told me that your mother said those were the two saddest words in the English language. Perhaps she was right."

After a while I heard the sound of hammering, and presently Matthew went down the garden and put a large wooden cross on the grave in which he had buried Rex. Then he went indoors, ate some breakfast and brushed his hair and, talking to me afterwards, said that Rex was three and a half years old and most rats only lived to four years. "But I shall never forget the way his little face screwed up when the vet injected him. It will haunt me all my life. It was so human. And people call rats vermin! How arrogant and ignorant we are!"

I put out a hand in the hope of comforting him, but he said: "No, no please, don't let's talk of it again. Let's talk of something else. What are we going to do with Cassidy? We've reprieved him; we've caused a stay of execution, but we've produced no permanent solution. And he can't live in this shed for ever. It's too small and he hates it. I heard him kicking around last night, and he's beginning to split some of the wood. Heaven knows what Meredith will say when he comes back next week."

"If only my mother had returned, she would know the answer."

"Is she a rider then?"

"No, but she's never short of ideas."

"Penelope is willing to buy him if necessary, on condition that some cure for his bucking can be found. She's been ringing around, but has no news of any stunt riders in this country. And one or two people are beginning to think she has a thing about cowboys."

"Perhaps Sir Stanley will understand," I said.

"You mean give the pony to you, and then a fairy godmother will come along and provide you with a field and money for his hay?"

"Perhaps my father," I began.

"Russians don't have English people's strange feelings about horses," Matthew said. "Look at that wren over there. No, stupid, by the magnolia. You don't often see wrens nowadays. Do you know, people used to think they were female robins?"

I looked and looked, but I couldn't see the little bird, only the ripening apples on the trees and the faded dropping magnolia blooms.

"You'll never make a naturalist," Matthew said.

"No, I'm more interested in the bigger animals," I replied, running my hand along Cassidy's back. "I loved that time we spent in the Fells, the black ponies, and the agile hill sheep and the sturdy bullocks. People think sheep are silly, but they're not. Lambs are very intelligent. Tropical fish, tiny birds, budgies and finches do not excite me."

In my optimism I felt that morning very poised and confident. No one, I decided, was going to put me off-centre, not even poor, dead Rex.

"I'll get the cards," Matthew said. "It's essential that you should learn to read quickly."

He came back with nine of them, having thrown out those on which he had written *Rex* and *Rat*. "I'm making some more," he told me. "Go on, call out the words on these." I remembered them all, except *Father*.

"Some significance there," said Matthew.

The new words he wrote were, he said, necessary to life. They were *hospital*, *doctor*, *love*, *like*, *hate* and *shop*. He read out each one in turn holding the card in front of him then, after shuffling them like a pack of playing cards, flashed them in front of my face in turn, saying, "Yes, come on, quick, what's the word."

"Good, you're learning very fast," he said eventually. "Perhaps you ought to teach me to ride or something. It seems wrong that I am always the teacher."

"I would if I had a rideable pony," I said.

Then the door opened and Penelope came across to us with Tao at her heels. "You look so companionable together," she said. "Listen, Sir Stanley has telephoned. We've had a long chat. I'm to send a signed statement to his lawyer that I accept full responsibility for Cassidy and for anyone he may injure in any way whatsoever. I'm drafting it now."

"Yes, does that mean he's ours?" asked Matthew, looking at me.

"Not yet. We are to discuss the whole question when he returns in four days' time. He's written to Smithers."

"Has he sacked him?" I asked with mixed feelings.

"No, he says he's too good a groom to lose in a hurry. Such men are hard to come by these days, so he's giving him a second chance. That's all really. Now we must find a cure for the pony, and a field too. Do rack your brains and solve that problem, while I go back to my legal document."

"Come on," cried Matthew, "what's that?"

"Like," I said.

"And that?"

"Shop."

"And this one?"

"Hate—— Now we must think about Cassidy," I said.

"So he's more important than reading then?"

"Not really. It's simply that his needs are more pressing at the moment."

"Oh, I hate pony-mad girls!" cried Matthew, laughing. "Perhaps it's just as well that I'm going away to a boarding school."

"I expect I shall miss you," I said. "Very much as a matter of fact. Why didn't you tell me before?"

"I kept hoping it would never actually happen."

"Poor you," I said, meaning it. "But now we must think about fields. Do you know any farmers?"

"I don't know," replied my friend, and suddenly his face was sad again and I knew that he was thinking about Rex.

CHAPTER SIXTEEN

A CELEBRATION

It was another of those tranquil, heart-warming mornings, with the sun dappling the grass from an azure sky lively with little darting clouds like sailing boats, tossed this way and that by an errant, undecided wind. I thought of the Fells again, of the grey crags which took on such strange shapes that sometimes, during that magical summer, I had been misled into thinking that people, or dead sheep or contorted monstrosities, awaited me in the hills behind Justin's farmhouse. The air there was different too, I reflected, the light softer than here in the Midlands. But what was the good of looking back? The idyll would now take its place in my memory as a special time, which was over for ever. "Never go back, always look forward," had been one of my mother's most frequent sayings as we moved on to other lodgings and other jobs.

I drew back the curtains as far as they would go, loving the first scents of the day. Everything, I told myself firmly, would turn out for the best. Bad times were usually followed by good ones. And I believed in twists of fate and gifts of providence. After all, it was as a result of my mother's trip to Russia that I had met Matthew. Even the saddest moments could suddenly lead to unexpected happiness. Picking up the Crown Infant Reader No. 1, I ran through the story that began "I am up on my ox" and the next one, and then stopped to wonder how my mother would feel about my reading. She had tried spasmodically to teach me, but had always lost patience, her mind too quick to stand my stumbling attempts to grasp the meaning of letters which presented no problems to children less than half my age. In this way she had unwittingly helped me to lose my self confidence, while struggling to be of use. "Oh, Katie, I can't bear it. Do you mind if we stop now?" she had cried, while the "p's" and "q's" and the "b's" and "d's" had continued to look the same to me, and much remained a blur of shapes I could not remember as separate entities. Now all that was ending. I was not stupid, after all, but could go on to lead an ordinary life like other young people. You need to have thought yourself hopelessly stupid to realize what this discovery meant to me, how it intoxicated me as, singing an Abba song, I ran across the garden to graze Cassidy before making myself coffee and toast. Hearing Tao's bold unmistakable bark, I wondered who would look after her when Matthew went to boarding school. (Dogs, I decided, were buffeted about by the winds of fate and the changing minds of adults as much as people like myself.) I wondered also whether Matthew would join me in the orchard this morning with his reading cards. How much did I care for him? How could I now face his impending departure to boarding school so calmly when sometimes a day without being with him seemed a day wasted? And wasn't I too young to become involved with anyone?

Arriving at the shed I thought for a moment that he had sawn the door in half at last, for I could see Cassidy looking out, his ears pricked in welcome, but a moment later I realized that the opening had been made by angry hoofs. Tired of being shut in, Cassidy had been beating his own way out. There was no need to bother Matthew or Penelope for the key. The plank that had held the catch was shattered. I went inside, and put on the halter. "Silly animal, idiot! I see your point. But . . ." I patted him despite my irritation, and he nuzzled me, as though he was glad of any company to break the loneliness of the night. "Yes, I know," I said relenting. "Ponies are not made for solitary confinement. We're driving you nuts. You don't need me, but another pony friend. You've had a miserable summer." I ran my hand along his back and

118

down his legs, checking that he wasn't hurt. There were no cuts, no swellings and no sign of abnormal heat.

Outside, Cassidy dragged me towards the orchard but, suddenly shy of Matthew and his reading cards, I took the pony instead to Patsy's garden where there was plenty of long grass near the field he had occupied until his removal to the slaughter-house.

I would graze him for an hour, I thought, and then Matthew would cut him enough grass to last until evening. Matthew was very quick and efficient with the sharp, sickle-shaped hook. I liked watching him work with deft strokes, bringing the grass down in swaths. Of course a scythe would have ben better and more beautiful, but in life it is often necessary to make do with what one has, I decided, becoming rather philosophical. While I mused about life, in this dreamy sort of way, a long white car drew to a standstill by Patsy's gate. A figure, dressed in jeans, a red shirt, with hair swept back and tied with a red kerchief, stepped out. There were amber beads at her throat and too many bracelets on her arms, and calling, "Katie!" she swung the gate wide.

"Mummy!" I shouted, rooted to the spot, holding Cassidy, seeing her anew, not as my mother, but as a young woman tanned by the sun and zestful with life, and much more elegant than I remembered her.

"You've got a pony then?" she came towards me with that long hip-swinging stride, her arms outstretched.

"He's not mine."

"The riding school's?"

She kissed me, and her flecked eyes took in my appearance. "You've changed. You've grown. You look more grown-up."

"I can read," I said. "And I have a friend called Matthew."

"Oh Katie! I'm so glad," she cried hugging me, "but now we are going to drag you away from it all. Is that awful?"

"No, I thought you might," I said. "We've just got to sort out Cassidy, that's all."

"Cassidy?" My mother's brows went up.

"The pony." I said, surprised by my lack of emotion. "Where are you dragging me?"

"Didn't you get my letter, explaining everything, about your father, and everything?"

"I couldn't read it," I began to blush and the hot feeling spread right across my body, down to my very feet.

"Didn't Patsy read it for you?"

"I lost it, before she had the chance."

"Oh Katie, dear Katie, Katerina, my love! So no one is expecting us?"

"No, but I can make you some coffee," I said. "I'll just tie up Cassidy. I expect we both have a lot of explaining to do."

"Do you remember Captain and Destiny?" asked my mother, smiling anxiously.

"Yes, but it all seems so long ago."

There was a bit of baling string on the palings which I had used before. As I tied Cassidy to this, I said: "What about us? I mean my father? Is he here?"

"Your new father. Oh Katie, I do so wish you had not lost that letter."

"Yes, but I know you were together in Roumania. Does he still have a black beard? We got the postcard."

"Oh yes, he does; he's sent you a birthday present, but Katerina, he's going to marry a Russian girl." My mother's bracelets jingled as she touched my arm. "Thirteen years is a long time for a married couple to be apart."

"So he isn't here? You haven't brought him with you? We are going back to our old life?"

Suddenly I felt miserable. "I ought to go to one school and stay there. I'm beginning to read, you see. Patsy has been so kind; she's been paying for intensive coaching and it works. I'm quite intelligent." My voice was a wail.

"Then I shall pay her back," my mother said, "and you shall continue your lessons. Look, look, turn your head, Katie, and see who's coming!"

It was a tall man with a weatherbeaten face, thick hair growing up from a widow's peak, and an open smiling face.

"Justin, Mr. Appleby! Did he fetch you from the airport?"

"He was in Roumania with me," my mother said. "My letter explained that he was coming out, so that we could get to know each other again, away from the farm. He has wanted to marry me for quite a time, Katie, but I was afraid that I wanted to accept him just for your sake, and it's not fair to marry a man for the sake of one's daughter. And I had to see Boris again to be sure that the old love had died. Do you understand? Do you see what I mean? Am I making sense?"

"I think so," I said.

"And I had to arrange a divorce. It is all so complicated if you are married to someone in the Soviet Union. You've no idea!"

Justin had stopped now and was watching us with concern, as though he was afraid that I had taken the news badly and resented him as a stepfather.

"She never read the letter. She lost it," called my mother. "I've had to put her in the picture."

"You never left an address. If you had, Patsy could have written and explained about the letter."

"Care of the British Embassy, Moscow, would have reached me. She knew that." My mother took my hand and led me to Justin.

"Hullo," he said, ruffling my hair in a gesture of awkward friendliness. "Will you come and live on the farm with us?"

"In the cottage again? I loved the cottage," I said, remembering the warm stone, the wind singing at night, the bleating of the sheep, and the lamb I had fed with a bottle.

"No, the big house, you can choose your own bedroom, so long as you leave the big one over the front door for us," said Justin.

"I'll have one at the back looking into the stable yard, please," I said. "A little one."

"We must get the decorators in. The place has grown shabby since my first wife died. We'll start anew, and you shall become manager of the stud of Fell ponies."

"Oh, I don't know enough!" I cried.

"Ah, but I have a sister-in-law who runs a fantastic riding school. She'll teach you, you'll see."

I thought of Miss Kirk and said nothing.

"That's a great pony tied to the palings," observed Justin. "Welsh, is he?"

"It's a long story," I said, "and terribly complicated. Come in and have some coffee and I'll fetch Matthew, and he'll help me to explain."

"And who might Matthew be?" asked Justin but, touching his arm, Mummy said: "Hush, darling, he's a friend from nearby."

"His parents are famous, film and television," I said, somewhat airily, suddenly aware that my life had not been so dull after all, and that I had, in retrospect, managed quite well without my mother. "I like them very much." I added. "They have a golden chow, called Tao, and a rat that died. They are not like other people, not ordinary at all."

"You are talking like your mother," said Justin, "and I like that. Do you reckon you can manage the ponies?"

"In time," I said, leading the way indoors.

My stepfather looked too large for Patsy's rather cluttered sitting-room, and, although he kept smiling, I had the feeling he was longing to get back to the farm.

"I've left everything in charge of my brother. He knows a bit, having been brought up there, but he's a lecturer on political economy now and rather out of this world, and I just hope he remembers about foot rot and everything. And I hope the dogs are all right."

"And the ponies," I added.

"Yes, and the ponies," he assured me. "We can't dally too long."

While Justin and my mother were drinking their coffee and eating some of Patsy's digestive biscuits, I fetched Matthew and together we told them all about Cassidy.

"My, what a saga," said Mummy.

"You sound just like my mother," remarked Matthew.

"Oh well, I suppose all mothers sound a little bit alike," sighed Mummy. "Now, Justin, what are we going to do about Cassidy?"

"Easy," said my stepfather. "I'll write a cheque out to Sir Stanley for one hundred pounds and we'll have him sent up to the farm."

"But he's no use; he's unrideable," I said.

"Oh, we'll soon change that."

"You must be a genius. How?" asked Matthew.

"First of all, we'll make a dummy rider and fix it so tight to the saddle that he can't buck it off, then I'll sit on him, and I don't think he'll buck very high with twelve and a half stone on top. And if that doesn't succeed, we'll break him to harness. You may remember, Katie, that I have a dinky little trap at the farm which will fit him very well. Well, some of the lanes round us are great for driving, and with those shoulders, he'll make a wonderful pony in harness. We'll win, Katie, one way or the other." He put his arm round me as he spoke and pressed me against him. "Who are the horse transporters round here?"

There was, of course, a good deal of sorting out to do, especially as Mummy and Justin wanted me to leave with them at once for Cumbria, and I hadn't even thought about it. But, after a lot of thought, Justin went to see Miss Kirk to arrange for board for Cassidy until he could be sent up to the farm. The fame of his first wife's stud of fell ponies had spread wide over the years and, unknown to me, Miss Kirk already knew of him and was surprisingly amicable. He said afterwards that her charges were much too high, but since Cassidy would be there only for a few days, they were bearable. Meanwhile my mother wrote a letter to Sir Stanley, enclosing the cheque, which she suggested he might care to give to the Hunt, if he found it unacceptable to himself. Then she rang Patsy, who closed her shop and came home bearing six pizzas, a bottle of Italian wine, some very superior ice cream and a large slice of Brie cheese.

"This is a celebration," she cried, kissing my mother on both cheeks with unusual warmth, as though she had never said a word against her. "Matthew, fetch Penelope. She must come too, and look, that wretched pony has escaped and is walking all over the garden. Oh, my poor Michaelmas daisies!"

"Better take him to Miss Kirk's straight away," advised my mother. Then seeing my reluctance, Justin offered to go in my place. "I expect Katie would like to help get lunch ready," he said, and I felt myself warming to him again, and his unfailing tact.

When he had gone, Patsy said: "Are you sure you're the right wife for a farmer? Won't you get terribly bored and restless?"

"Oh no," my mother cried. "It will be like going home. I loved that farm. I shall become a great midwife to the ewes, and I shall make my own bread and, I hope, rear more children out there on the fells. Patsy, that countryside is balm to the soul! At one moment I wasn't sure whether I was marrying for love of the farm or Justin. Now I know it's for both."

"But, if I may say so," Patsy began on a new tack, "you've been rather disgraceful in your neglect of your friend here."

"Of Katerina?"

"Her reading. You've neglected her schooling. The poor child! And apparently she's actually very bright. You should have let her stay in one place. Why, she tells me one year she changed school four times. She might have been a gypsy's child. Most irresponsible!"

"Patsy," said my mother. "Please don't spoil the celebration. That is now a thing of the past. Don't you see I needed roots myself, and now I've found them she will share in all that it entails."

"I'm all right," I said. "And Mummy did her best. I was just dim, that's all, and now I'm not."

After those few critical words, it was a very cheerful party with Penelope, Patsy and my mother all talking at once and interrupting each other. Then Mummy brought out some presents: a beautiful Roumanian mat for Patsy, a painted papier mâché Russian horse for me and, on the spur of the moment, a small bottle of vodka for Penelope. Justin gave to Matthew a collection of steel hedgehogs which fitted into each other to make a large ornamental hedgehog or separated into six little ash trays. A present which he must have meant originally for someone else. Presently Matthew and I went out into the Trumpingtons' orchard.

"It's all been very sudden," Matthew said. "But your

124

stepfather makes everything seem so simple. Do you have to leave within minutes?"

"Almost," I said. "If we had read that letter before losing it, we should have been well prepared. Justin says you are to come and stay on the farm whenever you like."

"What should I do? I don't know anything about sheep," said Matthew, looking suddenly despondent.

"Bring Tao and watch the wildlife."

"The two don't mix. And Tao's going to my aunt, who has just returned from America to take up residence with her academic husband in Oxford. They are supposed to keep an eye on me, too."

"It's all settled then?"

"Yes," agreed Matthew, putting an arm round my waist. "Do you want those cards as a sort of memento? Or do they embarrass you?"

"Yes, please," I said.

Pulling them out of his pocket, he handed them to me one by one with his half-mocking smile. "It all seems already like another world, a sort of fairy tale," he said.

"I'll send you a photograph of me with my perm," I said. "The new me. And one of Cassidy in his cart, or being ridden perhaps."

"I shall like yours best," said Matthew. "Katie of Cumbria! Now write down your address. Oh, sorry, you haven't got that far. Tell it to me."

"Your mother has it, don't worry, and I shall write for certain."

"I expect we shall both change. Nothing will ever be quite the same again," said Matthew. For a moment we looked at each other, searching for words we could not find, before I walked away to the big white estate car from which my mother was calling me. Matthew's voice followed me. "I should love to stay at half term," he said. "If that's convenient. Don't forget to write."

"No, I promise," I called, stepping into the car, afraid to turn because the sadness of parting always catches me by the throat, and I was determined to look forward in all senses of the word.

"Goodbye, Patsy. Goodbye, Penelope. A million thanks!" I cried in unison with my mother.

Justin accelerated gently; the car slid forward; the Lodge grew smaller. I had been so unhappy at times; yet now I didn't want to leave. I wanted a few more days to make the break, to adjust myself to the change and say a proper farewell. I felt as though I was leaving an important piece of myself behind, without due preparation, and yet I longed to see the Fells again and to know that something in my life was permanent at last.

"You've grown," my mother said, turning her head to smile at me from the front seat. "You've become a person in your own right."

"And I couldn't wish for a nicer daughter," added Justin, "and together we'll straighten out young Cassidy, you'll see. You can have one of Jessie's pups for your very own; she'll guide you home when the mists come down."

And so we drove on into the summer dusk and a new and different life.

DIANA PULLEIN-THOMPSON

*Three more exciting pony books in a thrilling series
by Diana Pullein-Thompson*

THREE PONIES AND SHANNAN

Christina Carr has everything most girls dream of: rich parents, a beautiful home with a butler and cook, an Irish Wolfhound puppy called Shannan, and three prize-winning ponies. She should be completely happy. But she isn't. She's lonely, and longs to make friends with the noisy village children on their rough, unschooled ponies. They, however, despise her.

How Christina stops being a spoilt little rich girl, goes to riding club camp and makes a friend for life is an engrossing and thrilling pony story.

A PONY TO SCHOOL

Christina and her friend Augusta are asked to school the skewbald pony, Clown. He is nervous and difficult, but they are determined to turn him into a happy, obedient mount. Then they discover why Clown's previous owners have failed to control him. The skewbald is a rearer – and if Christina and Augusta can't cure him of his dreadful habit, he will have to be destroyed . . .

ONLY A PONY

Alone while Augusta's mother is in hospital having a baby, Augusta and Christina stumble upon a pony who has been hidden in a stable by her young owner, Nico. Attempting to solve Nico's family problems and prevent his pony being sold, the two girls find themselves on the wrong side of the law and heading for danger.

Armada